The Bandit of Benson Park

Other books by Charles Mills

Though Bombs May Fall
Echoes of God's Love
The Shadow Creek Ranch series
Voyager
God and Me
Eyes of The Crocodile

The Bandit of Benson Park

Charles Mills

Pacific Press® Publishing Association
Nampa, Idaho
Oshawa, Ontario, Canada
www.pacificpress.com

Additional copies of this book are available by
calling toll free 1-800-765-6955 or visiting
http://www.adventistbookcenter.com

ISBN: 0-8163-1977-4

03 04 05 06 07 • 5 4 3 2 1

Dedication

To Dorinda, the girl who stole my heart

Contents

Chapter 1

Wild Animals

"Don't move," Alex whispered as he peered intently through the object held tightly in his hands. "Just a couple more inches and I've got him."

Shane and Alicia Curtain, laying on opposites sides of their friend, tried to press themselves further into the warm, grassy soil. "It's a big one," Shane whispered. "The biggest one around."

"Nah," Alicia argued, her freckled nose wrinkled slightly. "I've seen bigger. Just yesterday I almost hit one with my bike. Must have been . . ." the girl lifted her arms and held her hands about eighteen inches apart, "this long."

"That ain't nothin'," her brother countered with a frustrated frown. "I saw one . . ."

"Will you guys *please* be quiet!" Alex ordered as his fingers moved over the cool, metal surface of the device in his hands. "With all the noise

9

you're making, I'll be lucky to get a tail or ear. I want the whole creature with one shot."

"Creature?" Alicia giggled, brushing red hair from her eyes. "That's not a creature. It's just a dumb squirrel. Now, if you had your sights on a lion or even a wildebeest, that would be a creature."

Alex rolled his eyes. "And what would a lion or wildebeest be doing in the middle of Cyprus Hill? This is West Virginia. Not Africa. Use your imagination!"

The three remained silent for a long moment as they waited for their target to move into position. Overhead, a hot summer sun sparkled through the broad leaves of the tall oaks that sheltered the little park resting in the center of town. In the distance, the low rumble of traffic and *tap-tap-tap* of footsteps mingled with the gentle breezes.

"Nope. Can't do it," Shane declared.

"Can't do what?"

"I can't imagine that squirrel anything but a squirrel. A really skinny cat maybe, or a totally furry rat. But a lion or wildebeest? It just ain't happenin'."

At that moment, the animal sat up on its hind legs, sniffed the air, and then scurried away.

Click! The camera in Alex's hand responded to the quick pressure of his index finger. But even before the image had finished burning itself into the film resting in the dark cavity behind the lens, the boy knew he'd missed the shot. "Great. Another perfectly composed picture of grass. That squirrel was long gone before I could get my shot. Thanks, *partners.*"

"What did we do?" his companions gasped as he placed his camera back into its carrying bag.

"You ruined my picture, that's all!"

"Or," Shane said, "maybe it was that guy riding his bicycle down the sidewalk five feet away from your scary African creature that scared him off."

Alex glanced at the rider as he turned the corner opposite the antique shop across the street. "Well, maybe," he said. "But I can't yell at him. He's bigger'n me."

Alicia laughed. "Alex Timmons the wimp."

"You got that right," the boy admitted, turning his baseball cap back around so the bill would shield his eyes from the sun. Tufts of long auburn hair protruded over his ears and lay lightly on the collar of his shirt. "I choose to use my wits instead of my muscles, which is a good thing because I don't have all that many muscles."

"Well," the girl said warmly, "you're our favorite wimp. Besides, we wouldn't want a bully living next door to us."

The three stumbled to their feet, picking grass clippings from their bare knees. The effort left

Shane, who considered himself not fat but "weight challenged," slightly out of breath. His face and hair shared features common in his family—freckled and red. "We're no better off than when we got here two hours ago," he sighed. "We're supposed to take a picture of an animal in the wild. It's on the list. Mr. Cho said he'd give us two weeks to complete the assignment, and we've only got a week to go."

"What do we have so far?" Alicia asked.

Alex paused. "So far we've got great shots of an empty bird nest, an empty mouse nest, the left toenail of a crow, and the last three inches of a five-foot-long black rat snake."

Shane sighed. "Wild animals sure are fast."

"There's got to be a way of shooting a whole animal before it flies, scampers, or slithers away," Alex moaned as he took one last look at where the squirrel had been sitting. "There's just got to be!"

After walking a few paces, the trio arrived at the base of a tall statue rising up from a stone pedestal set amid carefully tended flowers at the center of the park. The three stopped and stared up at the bronze face of a determined-looking young man in a soldier's uniform. He seemed to be pointing at the bank building across the street. But they knew that wasn't the case.

"Harry Benson was a true hero," Shane called out, trying to mimic, word for word, the speech that the town mayor delivered on this spot every Veterans' Day. "It was a cold morning in Korea. Communist forces were pressing in on all sides. Our American boys were pinned down by enemy gunfire, cut off from help, hopelessly lost in the ice-covered mountains." Alex and Alicia sat down on a nearby bench to listen to their companion's energetic rendition of a story every citizen of Cyprus Hill knew by heart. "The smell of burning explosives and the flash of artillery filled the air. Suddenly, a voice could be heard above the din, a voice filled with hope and determination."

"This way, this way!" Alex shouted, jumping to his feet, picking up the saga with a shake of his outstretched hand. " 'I've found a mountain pass that leads back to friendly territory.' The soldiers turned to see Private Harry Benson standing amid the smoke and fire, in full view of the enemy, urging them to follow him to safety."

Alicia repeated the next part of the story. "And follow they did. That morning Harry saved his entire platoon from certain death. They made it back to the front lines before the sun set on that horrific day."

"But," Shane interrupted, clutching his chest in a dramatic gesture of sorrow, "Harry Benson of Cyprus Hill, West Virginia, wasn't with them.

He'd vanished in the smoke and flames, never to be seen again. That's why this statue stands tall and proud in the middle of our fair town. And that is why this park is named *Benson* Park. Harry Benson was a hero in every sense of the word. May we never forget his act of unselfish bravery and undying patriotism. AMEN!"

"Mayor Wilson doesn't say *Amen* at the end of his speech," Alicia said with a giggle.

"I know," Shane said. "I added that part myself."

Alex stood looking up at the statue, trying to imagine what it was like that cold day in a war-torn country so far away. "I wonder what happened to him," he said quietly.

Alicia shrugged. "Probably got blown to bits by an enemy hand grenade."

The boy reached into his bag and lifted out his little camera. "Might as well use up the last shot on this roll," he said, adjusting the lens for the proper exposure. "I might not be able to stop a wild animal in its tracks, but I certainly should be able to capture a statue that's been standing here for almost fifty years."

Click!

* * *

Kobe Myers looked up from his desk when he heard the knock on his second-floor apartment door. "I'm not here," he called.

"Yes you are," a voice echoed from the hallway. "I can hear your radio playing."

"I left it on when I went to the health food store."

"You're not at the health food store. I was just there, and they said you'd be in your apartment studying for a physics exam."

Kobe smiled as he stood and walked toward the door. "Sorry, but I'm not accepting visitors, unless you happen to be that annoying Timmons kid. Then, maybe, I'll make an exception."

"Must be my lucky day," Alex responded.

The door creaked open slightly. "Did you bring food?"

"Well," the boy hesitated. "I do have this half-eaten apple that I bought at the health food store. It's organic." He held the fruit up in front of him.

"Good enough." The door swung open fully, revealing an African-American young man dressed in blue jeans and a T-shirt with the words, "Heaven. Almost West Virginia" printed on it. The apple vanished with the wave of a hand, and Alex heard the soft crunch of eager teeth biting into it. "Make yourself comfortable," Kobe mumbled between chews, pointing at a small cleared area on the couch resting below a brightly lit window. Beyond the faded curtains lay Benson Park in full summer dress, its shaded walkways cool and inviting.

"So," the athletic-looking college student with the short-cropped hair and friendly eyes called as he returned to his study table. "What can I do for you?"

Alex sighed. "I can't catch any wild animals."

Kobe thought for a moment. "What trap are you using?"

The visitor dug into his bag. "This one," he announced as he pulled out his camera.

Kobe's eyebrows rose. "Oh, I get it. You're trying to take pictures of stuff like lions and tigers and they aren't exactly cooperating."

"Make that squirrels, birds, and snakes, and you've got the idea."

The older boy walked across the cluttered room and settled beside his visitor. "This is a pretty nice camera," he said, fingering the controls of the shiny device. "Bolsey Model D Twin Lens Reflex. Where'd you get it?"

"Internet. Only paid twenty bucks for it. Yeah, I know it's really old and stuff, but it takes pretty good pictures . . . of things that aren't moving."

Kobe lifted the camera up to his eye and squinted. "Thirty-five millimeter, nice split-field focusing screen. And check this out. Waist-level viewing with this flip-up viewfinder! Reasonably fast lens. Good aperture controls. Not bad at all."

Alex smiled. He liked impressing his older, wiser friend. Kobe attended the college that sat at the edge of town, and he worked part time at the health food store. But what Alex appreciated most about his companion was his keen interest in everything, even eleven-year-old boys with outdated photographic gear.

As Kobe continued to inspect the camera, Alex absentmindedly inspected the apartment. It was filled with its usual collection of electronic devices, "almost finished" inventions, and piles of books on every subject imaginable. In the center of the room rose a sturdy table supporting what was undoubtedly the most powerful computer in the county. Alex had always figured that if Kobe wasn't so disorganized, he'd probably be able to run the world from his little apartment overlooking the park. "So, why the interest in shooting wildlife?" he heard his friend ask.

Alex took the camera and held it proudly in his hands. "It's for my photography honor."

"Oh," Kobe said with an understanding nod, "Pathfinders, right?"

"Yup."

"Let's see, last month it was soil samples and planting schedules . . ."

Alex nodded. "For our gardening honor."

"In the spring it was butterflies and bees."

"Insects. I got stung twice."

"And around December you and your gang were out freezing your tails off studying . . ."

"Stars and constellations," Alex said with a pretend shiver.

The older boy grinned. "Well, I'm impressed. These honors that you earn, do you get a badge or something?"

"Yeah. Really cool ones! We sew them on the sashes we wear over our uniforms. I plan to collect every honor there is—me and my next-door neighbors Shane and Alicia. We've even formed what we call the Honors Club. Mr. Cho, our Pathfinder leader, lets us work on stuff just as fast as we want to. It's really lots of fun." The boy frowned. "At least it was until now."

Kobe thumbed his fingers on the coffee table as he thought for a moment. "Not fast enough, huh?"

"By the time I take my picture, the animal is in the next county. I'm getting frustrated. There are several squirrels in the park, and I can't even get one."

"Do you know what your problem is?"

"What?"

"When you get close enough to the wildlife to get your shot, they get scared and run away."

"Exactly."

"So, you either have to stay farther away, which you can't do because this isn't a telephoto lens, or you need to not be there."

Alex blinked. "How can I take a picture and not be there?"

Kobe stumbled through the piles of computer parts, the scattered innards of unrecognizable appliances, and unfinished robotic contraptions searching for something. "You need a mechanical you, something that can operate the camera without you." The young man paused. "And it needs to trigger the shutter only when something moves within its field of view so you don't waste film."

"You mean like remote control?"

"Better than that," Kobe responded, digging out a small battery-operated gadget from a pile of wires and circuit boards. "What you need is a triggering device run by a very sensitive motion detector."

"A what?"

The student lifted his hand. "You need this."

"I do?"

"You betcha. This little gizmo is the answer to your prayers."

"I really haven't been praying about it."

"I can retrofit this amazing little do-dad to work with your Bolsey. Do you have a flash attachment?"

"No."

"Not to worry, we'll use fast film."

"*Fast* film?"

"And when a wild creature like a squirrel or lion or elephant walks in front of the camera, this motion sensor here sets off this plunger, which presses down on the shutter of the Bolsey and, *ta-da,* you've got yourself a great photograph of nature at its most fierce and untamed. Any questions?"

"Ah . . ."

"You don't have to thank me. Just stop by this evening, and we'll get you set up in the park."

"This evening?"

"Sure. All good wild animal photographers take their best pictures at night when the jungle is teaming with critters."

"Really?"

"Absolutely. You and your friends be at the statue at nine o'clock sharp, and we'll get everything ready. The park will be empty, so no one will bother us. We'll position the camera in a tree where no one can see it and set it to fire at the slightest movement. Just make sure you get some really fast film."

"Yeah, I wanted to ask you about that. What do you mean by *fast* film?"

Kobe nodded. "Ever heard of ISO?"

Alex brightened. "Yeah. We read about it in the photograph book we borrowed from the library. ISO stands for International Standards Organizations. Each film is given an ISO number that means how sensitive it is to light, right?"

"Yup. The higher the number, the more sensitive, or *faster*, the film. At night, in the park, you'll need some very sensitive film, probably 800 or 1200 ISO. The street lamps will give us just enough illumination to light our prey. Check with the drugstore. I think they carry just the film you need."

"I make black-and-white pictures so I can develop and print them at the newspaper office," Alex stated. "Mr. Shepherd, the editor, has been teaching us how to use his equipment. It's really cool. If I don't get my wild animal, I'm going to go crazy! I really appreciate your help, Kobe. See you tonight."

As the boy left the room, the college student settled back into his chair and sighed a happy sigh. It felt good to share the knowledge he'd been collecting since he was a little kid growing up on the streets of Baltimore.

His friends all wondered why he'd chosen to further his education in a small West Virginia college town far from the city he knew so well. "And Kobe," they'd said, "Cyprus Hill ain't exactly the Black capital of the world." They were right. He hardly ever saw any African Americans in his part of the state. The ones who happened to amble by under his window were usually out-of-town tourists looking for antiques. No, he'd pulled up roots and replanted them in the small town not because he was running away from his past, trying to find something new, or hoping to explore a different cultural environment. Truth was, he simply liked West Virginia with its mountains and valleys, fresh-water rivers, and blue grass music. For Kobe Myers, that was enough reason to do anything.

From his window he watched Alex cross the street and skirt the park on his way to the corner drugstore. Noticing the big clock in front of the hardware store, he quickly turned his attention to the devise still held tightly in his hand. It would need a little adjustment in order to work as promised. And then there was the physics test scheduled for bright and early the next morning.

But, one thing he knew for sure. With the correct film and careful camera placement, his young friend would get the best wild animal picture ever taken in Benson Park.

Chapter 2

The Dark Hunt

Alex threw his cap and small bag of film onto the couch and headed for the kitchen where the familiar smell of warm tomato sauce and freshly baked muffins filled the evening air. His mother, Rose, a woman with carefully combed auburn hair and a faded apron covering her slender, petite frame, turned to see her son entering the cozy room. "Hey, handsome," she called, her blue eyes warm and welcoming. "Wash your hands. I've got beans."

The boy grinned. He *loved* beans. It didn't matter what kind. Baked, refried, boiled, tossed in soups, poured over rice, kidney, pinto, lima, garbanzo, or navy. If it was a bean, he'd eat it and ask for seconds.

"And what mischief did you get yourself into today?" his mom wanted to know.

"Nothing really exciting," Alex called from the bathroom over the sound of splashing water in the sink. "Tried to shoot a squirrel. Missed . . . of course."

Rose smiled. "Still can't nail any wild animals, huh?"

"Not a single one." Alex reentered the kitchen wiping his hands on his shorts.

The woman thought for a moment. "Why not take a picture of Marty?" she suggested, aiming a large spoon in the direction of the family mongrel lying by his food dish at the back door. "Maybe he could pass for a wolf." The animal pricked up an ear and tilted his head slightly to one side.

Alex chuckled. "Marty has a hard enough time passing for a dog," he stated. "I don't think I could make him look wild even if I used trick photography."

"Well," Rose continued as she placed two steaming bowls of baked beans on the table. "You'll figure it out. You always do."

"Actually, I'm getting some help from Kobe," the boy stated, seating himself beside his mother. "He's got some contraption he says will take a picture with my camera even when I'm not there. We're going to set it up in Benson Park tonight at nine. Should be interesting."

"How is young Kobe? Enjoying summer school?"

"I guess. He's really a good friend, and I like how he gets excited about stuff." The boy paused and cast a sideways glance at his mother. "It's nice to have a man around every once in a while when you need one."

Rose nodded.

"You know," Alex continued, "a strong father-type figure, male, nonfemale, kinda like a dad . . .?"

"I hear you," the woman stated.

"Yeah. A young boy like me needs to have that type of influence in his life."

Rose poured herself a glass of milk. "Message received loud and clear. You can stop harassing me now."

Alex grinned. "Speaking of influences and strong father-type figures, how's your boss, Mr. Shannon?"

"He's fine."

"Is he still the head librarian at the college, you know, where you're assistant librarian?"

"Yes, he is."

"And he's still single, as in unmarried and, like, totally available?"

"I believe so."

"Just checking."

"I appreciate that."

The two looked at each other and burst out laughing. This was a daily ritual, one that took place every evening at the supper table. Alex would leave hard-to-miss hints that he wanted a father, and Rose would do her very best to ignore him. But even as they giggled their way around the subject, the woman knew her son was right. He did need a father, almost as much as she needed a husband. But in a college town like Cyprus Hill, the male population seemed to be either far too young or far too old. Those who would fit the bill perfectly suffered from an incurable malady. They were already married.

"Say the blessing and eat your beans!" the woman ordered, trying to sound gruff.

Alex smiled and gently took his mother's hand in his. Together they bowed their heads, and the boy spoke quietly and reverently to the only Father he'd ever known.

* * *

Evening shadows lay long across the well-worn avenues and silent storefronts of Cyprus Hill. Streetlights flickered to life, lighting the way for Alex, Shane, and Alicia as they strolled to the center of Benson Park. They found a bench and sat down to wait for Kobe. Nearby, starry-eyed young couples, mostly college students, walked hand-in-hand below the oaks silhouetted against the darkening sky, whispering words of affection as daylight faded and night enveloped Cyprus Hill like a soft comforter.

Romance was the last thing on the minds of the members of the Honors Club. They had a job to do. They were on a mission! Somewhere, in Benson Park, a wild animal—known to the civilian population as a squirrel—waited to be captured on film. It was man against nature, human against beast, Pathfinder against rodent.

"Hey guys," Kobe called as he hurried to join the trio. "Great night for hunting. Full moon, warm breeze, light traffic. That squirrel is toast!"

"So," Shane said, eyeing the device held tightly in the student's hand, "how are we going to do it?"

"You just follow me and I'll show you," Kobe invited as the three got up and walked briskly behind their expedition leader. "See that big limb over there by the street lamp?"

"Yes."

"That's our hunting ground. We'll set the camera up on that smaller limb next to it and calibrate the motion detector to respond to the slightest movement. The street lamp will provide the light. What's the speed of your film, Alex?"

"ISO 1200."

"Outstanding! We'll be able to use a fast shutter speed, perhaps around 125th of a second and close the iris down to f5.6 or maybe even f8. Not only will we catch the wild animal in the act of being . . . wild, but we'll also be able to see a little bit of where the action is taking place—you know, the creature's natural habitat."

"How will we know what exposure to use?" Alicia asked. "Alex's camera isn't one of those point-and-shoot, automatic things. Mr. Cho said he wanted us to learn how to find and set the correct exposure on our own. So far, we've been following the directions written on the film boxes—you know, bright sunlight f16, open shade, f11, overcast, f8. Nowhere on the box does it say how to set a camera for a streetlight picture of a squirrel."

"Got you covered!" Kobe announced, lifting another device from his pocket. "This is an exposure meter—about as old as Alex's Bolsey. It measures the amount of light that's reflected off the subject. Here, I'll show you how it works."

The children gathered around their older companion and studied the object held snugly in his hand. It was about the size of a small box of candy. "You dial in the ISO of the film here," he said, following his own directions, "then you point the meter at your subject and press this button. Next, you twist this outer ring around until that pointer is positioned under that exposure needle and, bingo, you read your speed and f-stop combinations from these numbers printed in this window. Piece o' cake. Oh, and to make sure the camera holds steady, I've brought a little tripod to help mount it to the limb."

"This is totally cool," Shane said. "Let's do it!"

Within minutes, Alex's trusty Bolsey, tightly attached to Kobe's tripod, sat securely fastened with duct tape and rope to the tree branch facing the large limb. Kobe's motion detector and triggering device sat mounted above it, held in place by tape and string. Alex carefully sighted through the viewfinder to compose his shot, placing the top of the large limb—where the squirrel hopefully would be—along the bottom of the frame. In the background he could see the street corner, drugstore, and distant sidewalk. Next, he made adjustments for the proper exposure using the information called up to him by Shane who stood on the ground with Kobe's meter. Then to test the setup, he asked Alicia to toss a small twig up onto the large branch. On her third try, she placed it perfectly. As the twig hit the target area, Alex heard his camera go *click!*

"It works!" he shouted. "Hey, it works!"

"Of course it does," Kobe chuckled. "Now, reach over and put those peanuts I gave you on the big limb. Then wind the camera to the next frame so the shutter will be cocked and ready to go."

As the evening chill settled over Benson Park, Alex slipped down the trunk of the oak and joined his companions on the ground. They stood looking up at the camera. A few feet in front of the tripod waited the limb with a small pile of fresh peanuts serving as bait for their unsuspecting prey. The camera was loaded. The shutter was cocked. The trap was set.

"Well, I'll see you guys here tomorrow morning bright and early," Kobe announced. If the camera shutter has been tripped, we'll know we've got our shot."

"Oh," Alicia said with a shiver, "I don't know if I'll be able to sleep tonight. I'm so excited."

"Me, too," Shane added.

Alex just smiled. "Thanks, Kobe," he said.

"Sure thing, kid. See you guys at first light."

* * *

Few things in life can keep an eleven-year-old boy from sleeping soundly; a lightning storm, Christmas Eve, and waiting to see if he'd successfully captured a real wild animal with an ancient camera he'd purchased over the Internet. Alex tossed and turned, jumped at every sound, and got up repeatedly to stand at the window and gaze down the quiet street toward the distant park where his trap waited hidden in the tree branches. The moon shone full overhead, illuminating the lawns and houses with a soft, yellow glow.

The boy tried to imagine the scene in the park. A squirrel wakes up with the scent of fresh peanuts tickling its nostrils. It crawls out of its hole in the nearby tree trunk, scampers along, limb to limb, until it stands staring at a strange pile of fresh-roasted peanuts resting on a large branch by the corner under a street lamp. "Breakfast has come early," the animal reasons in his little squirrel brain. "I think I'll help myself!"

With that the creature ambles over to the feast and digs in, totally unaware that, just a few feet away a shutter has tripped, capturing his image for all time on a piece of high-speed film hidden in the dark recesses of a little, metal camera.

Alex closed his eyes, forming a mental image of the very instant the shutter snapped. Squirrel on limb reaching out one paw to retrieve his tasty prize. In the background stands the silent, midnight street corner with its empty sidewalks and dark storefronts. Awesome!

"It's not Christmas Eve."

The boy jumped as a voice sounded from the direction of his room door. He saw his mother standing silhouetted by the dim nightlight in the hallway. "Mom," he called out. "You scared me."

"Didn't mean to. If I wanted to scare you, I would have done this." The woman lifted her arms, curled the fingers jutting out of her bath-robe, and planted a twisted scowl on her face.

Alex laughed. "Oh, that would have been *much* worse."

Rose walked over and sat down on her son's bed. "So, partner, why the late-night vigil at the window?"

"Can't sleep," the boy confessed with a yawn. "Just wondering about my camera and the squirrel and whether it will work." He glanced over at his mother. "Why are you up wandering around?"

"Oh," the woman said with a sigh. "I was thinking about Mr. Shannon."

"Really?"

"Yeah. I dreamed that we got married and he insisted that I store all the food in the kitchen in alphabetical order."

Alex blinked.

"And I had to subdivide all our produce into food groups. You know, fruits in this section, vegetables over there, grains in one cupboard, nuts in another. Then I had to cross-reference the whole lot. It was a nightmare!"

The boy burst out laughing. "OK, OK, I'll stop bugging you about Mr. Shannon."

Rose chuckled for a moment, then her face relaxed into a sad smile. "I get lonely, too, you know."

"I know," Alex said quietly.

The woman stood and walked to the doorway. "See you in the morning," she called.

"Night, Mom."

Alex listened to his mother's footsteps as she shuffled down the hall and disappeared into her bedroom. He heard her door close quietly. Then the only sound drifting in the moonlit darkness was the soft ticking of the mantel clock in the living room.

* * *

"Alex. Alex!"

The boy's eyes blinked open.

"Hey, Alex. Let's go. It's morning."

Glancing toward the window, the would-be nature photographer noticed that the eastern sky glowed brightly with the promise of a soon-to-rise sun.

Alicia and Shane saw an excited face appear from behind the curtains of their friend's room. "I'll be right there," they heard him announce with a happy shout.

In minutes the three were racing at full speed, running along the still empty streets.

Even before they entered Benson Park, they could see Kobe standing at the base of the tree, gazing upward, hands thrust into pockets, a broad grin covering his face.

"I think we got one!" he called as the trio arrived. "My plunger flag is down, meaning that the shutter was triggered. Get up there, Alex. Check it out!"

The boy lost no time in scurrying up the trunk to the limb supporting his precious camera. Sure enough, an exposure had been made. While everyone was sleeping, or trying to, something had entered the scene and set off the motion detector. "We've got one!" he called down from his lofty perch. "Kobe Myers, you're a genius!"

"That's not genius," the student responded with a smile. "That's nature photography!"

Carefully, Alex lowered the equipment to the waiting hands of his friends, then joined them at the base of the tree. "Just think," he breathed. "We've got ourselves a real live wild animal captured on film."

"Or a falling leaf," Alicia said.

"Or a drifting piece of trash," Shane added.

"Nope," Alex insisted. "There was no wind last night, and autumn is still two months away. We've got ourselves a squirrel for sure."

Kobe detached the Bolsey from the tripod and motion detector. "Only one way to find out," he said. "You guys finish up this roll and then head for the newspaper office. I'm off to hunt for breakfast. Have a physics test today. Can't get an A on an empty stomach you know. Oh, and here, use my exposure meter for the rest of your shots. Just do like I showed you. Let me know what turns up on your negatives."

With a wave, Kobe headed in the direction of the little restaurant tucked in between two stores beside the bank just beyond the north boundary of Benson park.

"Come on, you guys," Alex called. "Let's finish up this roll before breakfast. Then we can develop the film at the newspaper office." He turned to Alicia. "What else is on Mr. Cho's shot list?"

"Let's see," Alicia responded as she pulled a crumpled piece of paper from her jeans pocket. "He wants us to photograph a tree and a flower, a rock formation, a moving object, and a picture of your best friend."

"That last one is easy," the boy grinned. "You guys go stand over there by that rose bush. Try to look natural and not posed. Be talking or something. And make it snappy. I want to finish this roll and get my wild animal picture enlarged to show Mr. Cho at our next Pathfinder meeting."

The two siblings made their way to the spot indicated by their young leader and stood trying to look like they weren't standing around waiting to get their picture taken. For the next thirty minutes, the three moved from place to place in the park, enjoying the soft, new light as it slanted past flowers, rocks, and early morning joggers.

One in the group would compose and shoot an image using the exposure information issued by another holding Kobe's meter.

They finished the twenty-fourth frame just as their stomachs reminded them that, in no uncertain terms, it was time for breakfast. "We'll meet at the newspaper office at nine-thirty," Alex suggested. "This is going to be fun!"

* * *

The noisy enclosure smelled of ink and old newsprint as Alex strolled into the office of the *Cyprus Hill Messenger,* the town's daily newspaper. The receptionist looked up from her computer and smiled. "Morning, Alex," she called.

"Morning, Mrs. Caldwell," the boy responded. "Is Mr. Shepherd here?"

"He's at an emergency meeting with Sheriff Curtain," the woman stated. "He told me to tell you to just go do your thing in the darkroom." The woman paused. "Hardly anyone goes back there anymore since we bought digital cameras for our regular reporters. Computers. They've taken over the world."

"Thanks," Alex called as he hurried past the piles of paper stock and printing supplies lining the hallway. He could hear the main press rumbling in another part of the building, spitting out the latest edition from its lair in the back room.

He entered a small enclosure formed by a large, circular metal tube that rotated when he pushed on the handhold. As it turned, it closed out the light and noise of the press-room and rotated the opening to reveal the entrance of the company darkroom. The chamber boasted a long sink, rows of shelves holding brightly colored boxes and jars of dry and wet chemicals, sturdy work areas with cutting boards and developing tanks, and a solidly built table supporting a tall, imposing enlarger. The enclosure was lit by a single bulb hanging overhead with a string dangling within easy reach. Other lights covered with yellow filters rested over the sink, the row of printing trays, and enlarger.

It hadn't taken the boy long to fall under the spell of a photographic darkroom. Within its dark confines he'd discovered a great sense of adventure. "Picture takers are never quite sure what will show up on their negatives," Mr. Shepherd had told Alex the first day he'd mentored him on the ins and outs of developing and printing photographs. "They have no idea what beauty will appear on the sheets of enlarging paper sloshing around in the tray. It's always exciting and fun."

Just as the boy finished assembling the proper chemical in the proper order for developing his film, the door cylinder rotated again, revealing the eager faces of his neighbors. "You're just in time," he announced. I'm going to load the film into the spool. Shane, get the lights."

His friend reached up and pulled on the string, throwing the room into total darkness. All other illumination had been switched off as well. The same light that forms an image on film through a camera lens can destroy an entire roll within a fraction of a second. Absolute darkness is required for moving the film out of its cartridge and into the developing tank.

Shane and Alicia heard their companion carefully remove the tightly wound roll of film hidden in the cartridge taken from the Bolsey and feed it into a developing spool. Before long, they heard Alex place the spool into the developing tank and close the lid. "She's ready," he called. "Lights, please."

Shane fished for the string in the darkness, and suddenly the room burst back into view.

One by one, chemicals were carefully poured into the tank. First the developer, then short stop, then fixer. Each step required careful timing and temperature control. The children worked silently, savoring their growing eagerness to see what the negatives would reveal.

At long last, after the film had been washed with running water for a number of minutes, they got their first view. Frame number one contained an empty branch with a small stick sailing by. "That was our test," Alex breathed.

Frame number two revealed that something, definitely something, was hovering over the pile of peanuts. "I can't tell what it is," Alicia cried. "Do you know?"

Shane squinted through a magnifying loop and studied the image. "It's hard to see since we're looking at a negative that shows dark areas light and light areas dark. Maybe we'd better make an enlargement."

"Good idea," Alex agreed. "I'll dry the negative, and we'll get to work."

Soon the three huddled around the bright glow of a greatly expanded image of the negative being projected from the enlarger towering over them. The main light had been switched off again. But, this time, the yellow lights fastened to the walls provided some illumination.

Alex carefully set the focus and the f-stop on the lens. Then he determined the proper exposure by running a test strip of one portion of the image, allowing the light from the enlarger to strike the different portions of the strip at four, eight, and twelve seconds. "Looks like we need around 8 seconds," he announced.

He set the timer, slipped an 8"x10" sheet of light-sensitive paper into the carefully positioned easel resting at the base of the enlarger, then stood back. "Ready?" he called.

"Ready," Shane and Alicia chorused.

Alex reached over and pressed the start button. The image appeared once again, this time projected on the photographic paper held tightly in place by the easel. "Four, five, six, seven, eight," Alicia whispered as she watched the timer count down the seconds.

Click! The enlarger lamp flicked off as the time ended. Alex retrieved the sheet of white paper and slipped it into the first tray filled with developer. Three sets of eyes stared down at the liquid. Three sets of ears listened to the soft *splash, splash, splash* as Alex rocked the container gently from front to back. Three sets of tongues remained silent as slowly, ever so slowly, a black-and-white positive image began to appear just under the surface of the chemical bath.

"I see the street lamp," Alicia whispered.

"I see the drugstore," Shane breathed.

"I see the tree limb," Alex encouraged, "and the big clock in front of the hardware store."

Then, just to the left of center, approaching the pile of peanuts, was a large, shadowy form. It had ears, a big nose, large thick body, and a tail."

"WE GOT HIM!" Shane gasped. "Look at that. It's our squirrel! We've got ourselves a . . ."

"Wait a minute," Alicia interrupted, leaning

closer to the developing image. "I don't think it's a squirrel."

"What do you mean?"

"Hey, you're right," Alex said, studying the image. "It's . . . it's too big and . . . too . . . hairy."

"Squirrels have hair, I mean fur," Shane insisted.

"Yeah, but all the squirrels in Benson Park have bushy tails," Alex said. "This tail is kinda . . . kinda . . ."

"Not bushy," Alicia announced.

Alex lifted the fully developed image out of the first tray and dropped it into the second. He counted out loud to ten, then carefully transferred the sheet to the third tray. After a minute had passed, he reached up and switched on the main light. Three heads pressed together over the photograph as it floated below the surface of the fixer.

No one spoke. The image was quite amazing in its detail. Beyond the limb rose a sleeping town, streetlights standing lonely above empty avenues and sidewalks. But, in the foreground, all they could see was a dark, shadowy blob that, with proper imagination, could be anything from a giant, thin-tailed squirrel to a mountain lion.

"My wild animal is totally out of focus," Alex moaned as the bright light overhead revealed the picture's secrets in vivid detail.

"How can that be?" Shane said. "Didn't you focus the Bolsey right before you climbed down from the tree?"

"Yes. I put the little pile of peanuts on the limb and then checked the focus. The drugstore was perfectly clear."

"The drugstore?" Alicia gasped. "You focused on the drugstore?"

"Well, yes. It's what I could see the best."

"But we wanted to take a picture of a squirrel *eating* peanuts, not shopping for them. You should have focused on the spot where the squirrel would eat."

"There was nothing there!" Alex countered. "How am I supposed to focus on something that's not there?"

"Good point," Shane said with a nod.

Alicia's mouth opened as if ready to say something, then she fell silent. "Hum. You're right, Alex. It's pretty hard to focus on nothing."

The boy sighed. "Whatever I did, it wasn't what I was supposed to do. We've got a great shot of downtown Cyprus Hill at . . ." he checked the time showing on the clock in front of the hardware store, "at three thirty-seven in the morning framed by a great big blob of some weird creature. Some nature photographer I am."

"The big blob that ate Cyprus Hill," Shane said with a chuckle. "Maybe we can make a movie."

Alex sighed. "I don't believe this. We're *never* going to get our shot of a wild animal. Maybe Mom was right. I should just take a picture of Marty."

"That mutt?" Alicia giggled. "Maybe if we dressed him up in a werewolf costume from Halloween."

"One thing's for sure. We've got to try again, and somebody's got to explain to me how I'm supposed to focus on something that's not there." Alex sighed. "Come on, you guys, let's print the rest of our negatives. Maybe we've got some shots that will work for Mr. Cho's list. We'll have to try again tonight to capture our creature in the wild. I hope Kobe has time to help us. I also want him to explain to me how to focus on something that's not there."

The three sighed and turned their attention back to the enlarger and the other negatives waiting on the roll. All wasn't lost, they agreed. At least some creature that lives in Benson Park had enjoyed a late-night snack of fresh-roasted peanuts.

Chapter 3

Shadow Image

Sheriff Curtain and Mr. Shepherd were just entering the newspaper office as Alex, Shane, and Alicia exited the darkroom. "Hi, Dad," Shane called.

"Hi, kids," the sheriff responded with a smile. "Did you get your squirrel?"

"Well, we got something," Alicia stated, "but we aren't sure exactly what."

Mr. Shepherd lowered his trim, some would say "skinny," body onto his desk chair and started rummaging through some papers. "Seems we've got two mysteries in town," he said, adjusting his wire rim glasses and scanning a police report selected from the pile.

"Two mysteries?" Alex said.

The editor nodded. "Last night someone broke into the hardware store. Stole about four hundred dollars worth of merchandise."

"Wow," Alicia gasped. "Maybe he's the one who ripped off our peanuts too."

Alex chuckled. "I don't think that's a person up on that limb."

Sheriff Curtain sat down at the edge of the desk, causing it to creak. He shared his son's propensity to being slightly overweight as well as his crop of shiny, red hair. "This isn't the first time the town's been hit," he stated with a sigh. "Last week someone broke into the gas station by the elementary school. Week before that, the antique store on Mercer Street was relieved of the contents of its under-the-counter safe. This guy knows what he's doing. He knows where valuables are kept. I'd say he's a local."

Mr. Shepherd nodded. "I agree. This thief is smart. He or she knows the best time to strike. The gas station job took place in the evening after closing time. The antique shop break-in happened while the owner was eating lunch right next door in the restaurant, and the hardware store hit went down in the dead of night. The silent alarm sounded at our station at exactly three forty-one. My deputies got there as quickly as they could, but the guy was long gone."

Alex frowned. "What time did you say that alarm went off?"

Sheriff Curtain double-checked the notes he'd scribbled on the small pad of paper he always carried in his back pocket. "Like Mr. Shepherd said. Exactly three forty-one in the A.M."

The children looked at one another, then back at the two men. Sheriff Curtain leaned forward. "Is . . . is something wrong?"

Shane cleared his throat. "Well, we kinda have something you might want to see."

"Yeah," Alicia added. "It may not be anything. But . . ."

"What is it?" the sheriff asked.

Alex fingered the large envelope he was holding. "We . . . we kinda have a picture of the street corner and drugstore taken last night . . . at three thirty-seven."

Mr. Shepherd blinked. "You what?"

"We had my camera set up to take a picture of a squirrel using a motion detector Kobe Myers let us use. Alicia, Shane, and I are working on our photography honor for Pathfinders. Anyway, some animal, we're not exactly sure what kind it is, tripped the shutter at exactly three thirty-seven—that's the time showing on the clock outside of the hardware store. You can see the clock because I focused on the wrong thing. Maybe the thief was in the area when the picture was taken, and maybe he's in the shot somewhere although we didn't see anything when we printed it."

The sheriff glanced at the editor and then back at the children. "May . . . may we look at the photograph?"

"Sure," Alex said, opening the envelope.

Five sets of eyes hovered over the image as soon as it was laid down on Mr. Shepherd's desk. Alex cleared his throat. "That's our mystery creature right there," he said pointing.

Except for the unrecognizable blob on the left side of the picture, the night scene was actually quite beautiful. Everything in the background was clear and well defined. The drugstore stood facing the park from across the deserted street. Next to it rested the hardware store, a small restaurant, and one corner of the bank. Street lamps spilled bright pools of light on the scene, revealing the rough, worn texture of each brick and length of wood. A discarded newspaper leaned against a curb, and a soda can lay where it had been tossed on the sidewalk.

Then, those five sets of eyes saw something else, something not immediately apparent at first glance. In the shadows, between the restaurant and hardware store, stood a lone figure, its outline almost lost in the light and dark blending of the image. It was easy to miss. Unless someone was actually looking for a person in the scene, he or she would pass it off as just an odd arrangement of shadows. But, the two men and three children gazing down at the image knew there'd been someone in that area at almost the same time indicated on the hardware store clock.

"I don't believe it," Sheriff Curtain whispered.

"Amazing," Mr. Shepherd gasped.

The police officer straightened and glanced over at his companions. "You young people may have accidentally taken a picture of a wanted felon about to commit a crime. I'm afraid I'm going to have to confiscate both this enlargement and its negative. They may be useful as evidence in a trial."

Alex nodded and pointed down at the image. "We can enlarge that portion of the picture where the person is standing. Maybe you'll be able to tell who it is."

"My thoughts exactly," Mr. Shepherd agreed. "Let's do it right now."

This time, as the group entered the dark-room, the young people weren't filled with their usual sense of adventure. Their earlier excitement had vanished, replaced by a cold, unfamiliar fear. Unknowingly, they'd photo-graphed an unsavory person about to break the law. Even more chilling was the fact that, perhaps, it was someone they knew. Maybe it was the checkout man at the grocery store or the woman who handed them candy samples at the Sweets Shop on Mercer Street. And even more unsettling was the thought that maybe that person had seen them retrieve the cam-era at dawn and knew he or she'd been caught in the act of being in the wrong place at the wrong time!

As Alex positioned the negative in the holder, and then slipped it into the enlarger, he found that his normally steady hands were shaking ever so slightly.

As soon as the lights had been turned off, he rotated a lever on the enlarger, sending the apparatus's head higher and higher, creating an ever-expanding image on the easel below.

"I think that's the best we can do, Alex," Mr. Shepherd told his young friend. "The high-speed film you used is very grainy. It's not good for making big enlargements. Everything gets fuzzy."

The sheriff leaned over and studied the negative image outlined by the easel. "That should do it," he said softly.

Shane retrieved a sheet of photographic paper from its light-tight box under the counter, and before long another picture was fading into view in the first tray. Once the developing process had been safely halted in the short stop tray, the paper was quickly lowered in the fixer bath in order for it to lose forever its sensitivity to white light. Then, the main light was switched on again.

Sheriff Curtain leaned low to examine the print with a magnifying glass in hand, his fingers almost touching the fixer. "Looks like a white male, but . . . I don't recognize him," he said, moving the glass across the image, looking for clues to the stranger's identity. "It's not clear enough to get an age estimate or to see any identifying feat . . ." The children saw the magnifier stop suddenly.

"What is it, dad?" Alicia whispered.

The man straightened and handed the glass to Mr. Shepherd. "Look . . . there," he said pointing into the liquid.

The editor bent and studied the image. Then he rose, his brow furrowed into deep lines of concern.

"What's the matter, Mr. Shepherd?" Alex asked. "What do you see?"

"We've got a problem," the man said, deep in thought.

"We certainly do," the sheriff agreed.

Without saying another word, the two men exited the darkroom.

Alex, Shane, and Alicia stood staring at the door opening as it rotated, leaving them alone in the chamber. Shane reached over, picked up the magnifying glass, and bent to examine the image that had caused two men to suddenly grow quiet. He saw the grainy, somewhat blurred face of a man. Moving down the figure he came to the stranger's side where he noticed a hand resting by a jacket pocket. In the hand, almost hidden by the shadows, was a gun.

* * *

Kobe Myers looked up from his computer as Alex timidly entered the apartment. "Hello, young Timmons," the student said with a smile. "How'd our picture come out?"

Alex grinned sheepishly. "Well, there's good news, bad news, and really bad news."

Kobe frowned. "What do you mean?"

"I mean that we did get a picture of an animal about to eat our peanuts."

"Animal? You mean squirrel?"

"Ah . . . no, just animal. We're not sure what it is."

Kobe shook his head. "Maybe you'd better show me what you're talking about."

The visitor opened the large envelope he was carrying. "This is an 8"x10" of frame number two. It's the second full enlargement I made of it."

"Second? Where's the first?"

Alex hesitated. "That's the bad news. I had to give the photograph and the negative to Sheriff Curtain."

The student blinked. "The sheriff? What did he want with your picture?"

"That's the *really* bad news. He wants them as evidence."

"Evidence for what?"

"Here, I'll show you." The young photographer walked to the computer desk and placed the enlargement over the pile of opened books lying by the keyboard.

"Whoa!" Kobe said with a chuckle. "That's one out-of-focus critter. Something tells me you didn't set the camera correctly."

"Yeah, I know. But look right . . . here." Alex placed his index finger over the dark space between the restaurant and hardware store. "What do you see?"

Kobe studied the image for a long moment. "A really lonely-looking person standing in the shadows at three thirty-seven in the morning?"

Alex nodded. "Just a few minutes after this picture was taken, the hardware store was robbed."

The student let out a long, low whistle. "And the sheriff thinks this person did it?"

"Maybe. But, there's something else. When we blew up that portion of the frame, we found that the person was holding something in his hand."

Kobe's eyebrows rose. "A . . . whiskey bottle?"

"No."

"Bus schedule?"

Alex chuckled. "No. A gun."

The student's face paled. "A gun? Are you telling me that there was someone wandering around the street last night with a gun in his hand?"

"Yup. And I wanted to try to get another picture of that . . . that . . . whatever it is in the park tonight, but Sheriff Curtain says he's going to put up a sunset-to-sunrise curfew on the whole town until this weirdo is caught. He doesn't want us kids wandering around outside in the evening either. I heard him say to Mr. Shepherd that there's no telling what this crazy guy might do. He could be spaced out on drugs or drunk as a skunk." The boy shivered. "Makes me a little nervous."

Kobe sat staring at the photograph for a long moment. "One of the reasons I left the city was to get away from this type of thing," he said quietly. "Seems bad stuff can follow you no matter where you go."

Alex sighed. "All I know is that we won't be able to complete our assignment for Mr. Cho and get our photography honor for a while."

"Pre-focus," Kobe said.

Alex turned. "What?"

"You didn't pre-focus the camera. That's why the animal is blurry."

The boy settled into a nearby chair. "Yeah, I wanted to ask you about that. When we set up the shot, I focused on the only thing I could see clearly . . . the drugstore. That was a mistake."

Kobe shook his head. "No, you didn't make a mistake. You just didn't know the correct way for setting up the picture. You see, since the squirrel was going to be on the limb, you needed to set your focus to match the distance from the camera to the limb."

"It was kinda dark," Alex said. "I couldn't see the split focus in the viewfinder unless I was looking at the drugstore."

"But," the student continued, leaning forward in his chair, "there is something you could have seen using your flashlight—the feet-to-subject numbers on the lens. Since the limb was around four or five feet away, you could have set the focus using the four-foot indicator on the outer ring of the lens. That's called 'pre-focusing' for a picture. Basically, you'd be focusing on . . ."

"Something that's not there!" Alex gasped. "I didn't think you could do that."

"Sure. Then when this . . . this . . . whatever ambles into frame, the camera would be set to capture him clearly, totally in focus."

Alex thought for a moment. "Pre-focus, huh?"

"That's the answer."

The boy shrugged. "Oh, well, I won't get a chance to use it since we're not supposed to go into the park at night. And I already know that I can't shoot a squirrel in the daytime. When I get close enough, they run away." He sighed. "What am I going to do?"

Kobe thought for a moment. "All is not lost, my sad and worried friend." He stood and walked to the window. "What do you see out there?"

Alex joined him. "I see Benson Park."

"Then you will continue your hunt from this very window."

The boy laughed. "I appreciate your offer," he said. "But my little Bolsey only has a wide-angle lens, which is great for taking pictures of buildings, entire forests, and the Grand Canyon. From here, any wild animal I photograph would look like a tiny speck in the frame . . . a little dot lost in all of those leaves."

"You're right," Kobe responded. "But what if I told you that, since I'm a physics major and my professors think I'm a genius—which I guess I am— I could borrow from the college a special camera that, not only will allow you to shoot squirrels from a distance, but you can also take your pictures in the dead of night!"

Alex blinked. "No camera can do that."

"Oh, but you're wrong, young Timmons. Tell you what, ask your mom if you can spend the night here, and we'll capture that critter without even breaking a sweat."

"Really?"

Kobe grinned. "Hey, I want you to get this honor as much as you do. Then maybe you'll leave me alone and let me get some studying done."

Alex ran to the door. "I'll be here," he called over his shoulder. Then he paused. "What type of film should I get this time?"

"Film?" the student responded, laying his hand on the top of the big monitor hovering above his keyboard. "Who said anything about film?" Alex's eyes opened wide. "Wow. OK. I'll be here around six. Thanks, Kobe."

"And bring food!" the young man called. "Pizza. With lots of cheese."

"You got it!"

Kobe walked to the window and watched his energetic friend race down the sidewalk. He smiled, remembering what it was like to be a child facing an unknown adventure. During those years in the city, when someone offered to help him with a pressing problem, especially an older person, he believed that anything was possible.

The student's gaze returned to his computer desk and the enlargement lying across his home-work assignment. "Who are you?" he asked the shadowy image of a man standing by the hardware store. "And why are you bringing such fear into my town?"

* * *

"But, Mom, he'll think I'm a little kid."

"You *are* a little kid."

Alex sat down heavily on the couch and crossed his arms over his chest. "I'll be safe in Kobe's apartment. I won't set foot outside until morning! Besides, it's been three days. He keeps calling and asking when I'm going to come over and try to get another wild animal picture, and I keep having to tell him that my mom won't let me out of the house."

Rose pressed her gurgling iron even harder into the fabric of her jogging pants. "Alex, there's a guy with a gun running around Cyprus Hill at night! I'm not about to let you out of my sight, especially when it's dark. It's just not going to happen."

The boy sat silent for a moment. "If I had a dad, he'd let me stay over at Kobe's," he said with more anger than he'd planned. Even as the words left his lips, he knew he shouldn't have said them.

Rose closed her eyes and lifted the iron slightly. "That's not fair," she said.

Alex sighed. "I'm sorry, Mom. It's just . . . it's just that Kobe teaches me stuff, fun stuff. I like being with him."

The woman glanced over at her son. "This isn't about Kobe. Yes, he's great. He's God's gift to eleven-year-old boys! I like him too. But there's some idiot sneaking around the shadows carrying a deadly weapon. You saw the picture in the paper, didn't you?"

Alex laughed. "Mom, I *took* the picture in the paper, or at least my camera did, thanks to Kobe's motion detector."

The woman softened. "Did I tell you how proud I am that you got your photograph published? Everyone thinks you're wonderful, including me."

"What everyone didn't see is my totally amazing shot of an out-of-focus animal," Alex stated with a grin. "I'm glad Mr. Shepherd cropped that part out when he printed my picture. I wasn't even trying to get a photograph of a man with a gun. I was going for a squirrel with a peanut!"

Rose lifted the jogging pants out in front of her and inspected her work. Then she lowered them to her side and held them at her waist. She was about to say something to Alex when he called, "No, Mom, they don't make you look fat."

The woman smiled. "Good boy."

"Mom. Kobe? Tonight?"

Rose placed the iron on its holder. "Kobe lives in Mr. Anderson's apartment building, right?"

"I guess so. It's the one right across from the park."

"I just remembered that Trisha Scaggs, Mr. Shannon's secretary, lives there too. Maybe if I give her a call and she says it would be all right, I could stay with her while you go big-game hunting with Kobe."

Alex's eyes opened wide. "You mean it?"

"We'd at least be in the same building, and I wouldn't worry so much."

The boy jumped up from the couch and landed with his arms around his mother. "Oh, that would be *so* cool. Could you call her right now so I could let Kobe know I'm coming tonight? Could you?"

Rose smiled. "Well, I would except I have this crazed child hugging me so hard I can't breathe."

Alex released his grip. "You're the best, Mom, the very best. Oh, and while you're on the phone, you can order some pizza . . . and salad . . . and soft drinks for Kobe and me. Hunting big game from an apartment window can give guys a really big appetite!"

The woman nodded. "Pizza, salad, and soft drinks. May I have a slice when it's delivered?"

Alex grinned. "Just one. It's going to be a long hunt."

* * *

As night enveloped Benson Park, the curtains covering Kobe's window overlooking the small expanse of oaks and grass parted, revealing two eager faces, one white, one black. Behind them, resting on a large, sturdy tripod, sat a state-of-the-art digital camera connected with a thin cable to the computer humming quietly on the table in the middle of the room.

Kobe had spent the entire evening explaining how the system worked. "High-resolution images captured by this extremely light-sensitive camera will be sent to my computer," he'd said with Alex drinking in every word. "In the computer, a software program will translate the data into colors and shapes, throwing them up on the screen and making them available for printing at the press of a button. The military uses this type of high-tech device to spy on bad guys. So, think of that squirrel as enemy-number-one. You're the United States Army!"

Several piles of peanuts had been strategically placed throughout the park in full view of the camera boasting the biggest, meanest-looking telephoto lens Alex had ever seen.

The boy grinned. His friend Kobe had come through on his promise once again. Being the darling of a college physics department certainly had it perks! Now it was up to luck and his steady aim to capture the after-dark activities of whatever creatures roamed Benson Park.

Slices of pizza and cans of soda pop waited nearby, ready to dull the appetites and quench the thirst of the two intrepid hunters.

Tonight would be the night. Alex just knew it. If anything so much as moved among the darkening trees or scurried across the carefully clipped lawns below, he was ready. With Kobe at his side, everything was possible!

Chapter 4

Long Arm of the Law

Alex wasn't sure what woke him. He'd been happily hunting a rogue elephant in his dreams, shooting frame after frame of the enraged animal from the safety of his jungle tree house. Then, he was awake, lying on Kobe's couch listening to the quiet hum of the student's computer.

The boy yawned, filling his lungs with the cool night air drifting through the open window. A glance at the digital clock resting atop the bookcase revealed that his "short nap"—as he'd described his need to take a break from his park vigil—had turned into a four-hour snooze. It was three A.M.

Blinking sleep from his eyes, Alex rose, walked stiffly to the window, and settled himself beside the tripod. The steady buzz of crickets filled the air, their drone mingling with the occasional dog bark echoing from somewhere in the distance.

Both the street and park wore the snug, dark cloak of night, whose shadowy folds reluctantly gave way to the forced intrusion of streetlights. There was an almost unnatural look to the scene, like some artist had painted Cyprus Hill and its little patch of green using far fewer colors than usual. Black, white, gray, silver, and a hint of yellow seemed to be the hues of choice.

Alex positioned himself behind the camera and squinted through the viewfinder. Even more colors faded away as the night-vision technology housed in the device amplified whatever light it found and rendered it in clear but monotone shades of green and white.

Through the camera's unblinking eye, the boy saw the outline of trees, the winding sidewalks, even the grass covering the lawns. "If there's light, any light at all reflected by the subject," Kobe had said, "this awesome device will pick it up. It won't look like daylight, and it won't look like night either."

Suddenly, a small animal raced through the image in the viewfinder. Alex stiffened. "What was that?" he breathed quietly to himself. "I think Mr. Squirrel is smelling those peanuts." He panned the camera to the left. Sure enough, there on the lawn sat the bushy-tailed creature he'd been hunting for days. The boy held his breath as the index finger on his right hand reached for the shutter release. But, before he could press it, the animal moved on.

"Ahhh!" Alex whispered. "Stay put, critter!"

He followed the ambling creature, keeping the animal's image in the viewfinder. "You mustn't be moving the camera when you take your picture," Kobe had warned. "Shoot when everything is locked off, when you're not panning or zooming."

The squirrel continued to walk/hop/jump/ stroll across the lawn, pausing just long enough to scratch himself. Sometimes he'd vanish behind a clump of leaves then reappear as he continued his late-night trek through Benson Park.

"You're mine," Alex whispered repeatedly. "I'm not going to let you out of my sight until I get a good shot. So STAY STILL!"

As the animal passed the center of the park, it hesitated by a bench and scratched himself behind the ear. Once again, the young cameraman's finger quickly moved to the shutter. But before he could fire the camera, the animal moved on. That's when the boy noticed something strange in the background, just behind where the squirrel had paused. Alex squinted, trying to make out the unusual shape that filled his viewfinder. Then, one of the mysterious objects moved slightly.

"What in the . . ."

Alex's words caught in his throat as he suddenly recognized what he was seeing. The strange objects weren't rocks or bushes. They weren't clumps of grass or leaves. They were boots. Two boots. And they weren't empty.

The boy reached up and tapped the zoom control on the long, thick lens. Slowly, the boots moved away slightly as the image widened to include the right portion of a park bench. Tapping the control again, the scene pushed back even more, revealing the entire bench and part of its surroundings. Alex gasped. There, sitting on the bench facing the towering statue, was a man, his shape clearly outlined by the light-enhancing power of the lens.

Click. Without thinking, Alex pressed his index finger down on the shutter release. He heard the camera beep once, then twice, indicating that it was ready to fire again. Behind him, the image of the man sitting on the bench scrolled onto the computer monitor.

"That must be the bad guy," Alex breathed aloud, "the man in the shadows, the crook that broke into the hardware store."

"What are you mumbling about?" The boy jumped as Kobe stumbled into the room, yawning.

"Kobe!" Alex whispered, his voice shrill and airy. "Look at the monitor. Look at the monitor!"

The student seated himself in front of his computer rubbing his eyes. "Did we get the squirrel?" he asked.

"Does that look like a squirrel?" Alex responded excitedly.

When Kobe focused on the image glowing on his screen he blinked, unsure of what he was seeing. Then reality hit him like a cold wind. "Whoa!" he gasped. "Is he there now?"

"Yes!"

The student grabbed the phone from its cradle and hit speed dial one. Alex heard the muffled tones of the number being rapidly dialed, then his friend spoke into the handset. "Hello? Yes. This is Kobe Myers. There's someone in the park sitting on the bench by the statue. Might be the man you're looking for, you know, the guy with the gun. Yes, he's still there."

Click. Kobe heard the camera fire again. This time when the image appeared on the screen in front of him, he noticed that Alex had zoomed in for a close-up of the man's face. He threw a quick thumbs-up to the young shooter at the window as he hung up the phone. "They're on their way," he called. "Keep him in view. Don't let him out of your sight!"

Alex nodded, tightened his grip on the camera body, and squinted into the viewfinder studying the face that filled his field of vision. Even with the extreme processing taking place on the image, he could see that it was the face of an older man, kinda like the janitor at school. But this wasn't the janitor. This man had different eyes, and his jaw wasn't as jagged.

Alex began to feel a little unsettled. There was something familiar about that face, as if he'd seen it before. The curve of the nose, the tilt of the chin, the eyes. Maybe it had been a picture in a magazine or book. Perhaps a news report in Mr. Shepherd's paper. The boy shook his head as if to clear his thoughts. Nah. He was imagining things. This guy was a stranger, someone who didn't belong in Benson Park at three o'clock in the morning.

Alex stepped back from the camera and moved to the monitor where his last image glowed in the darkness, revealing a feature he hadn't fully noticed in the viewfinder. The stranger sitting on the bench looked . . . sad.

The two hunters heard a car door close and footsteps echo on the street below. Returning to the camera, Alex aimed the lens at the entrance to the park. Two deputies, pistols drawn, entered Benson Park. The boy at the camera and student at the computer watched the officers move through the shadows, getting closer and closer to the unsuspecting visitor.

Alex positioned his finger on the shutter and waited, zooming out to include the bench and surrounding trees. Then, with a distant shout, the deputies rushed the man, one from the front, one from the back. *Click.* The old man jumped to his feet, frightened by the sudden appearance of the police officers. *Click.* One officer shouted, his commanding words disturbing the stillness of the silent town. "Freeze! Don't move!" *Click.*

The stranger turned to run but was immediately tackled by the second officer. *Click.* There was a short scuffle as the two police officers pinned the struggling man to the ground, kneeling on him in an effort to subdue his wildly thrashing arms and legs. *Click. Click.* It was over in less than thirty seconds, and the two officers led their captive out of the park.

Alex and Kobe watched the three men cross the street, enter the police cruiser, and drive away.

Kobe ran to the computer and entered some commands, saving the images to the hard drive. He opened another program and began burning the picture files onto a CD. "That was amazing!" he breathed, shaking his head in disbelief. "Alex, you got some absolutely awesome photographs of a totally bad guy getting caught by the long arm of the law." He pointed toward the window. "I think you just shot the ultimate wild animal in Benson Park."

Kobe glanced over at his young friend. "What . . . what's the matter?"

Alex stood looking out toward the now silent street. The crickets had stopped singing, their reverie disturbed by the violence of the arrest. "He looked so sad," the boy said softly.

"Of course he looked sad. He just got nailed by two of Cyprus Hill's finest."

"But," Alex continued, "where was the gun? He didn't have a gun."

"Maybe he stashed it somewhere. Besides, who cares? The mystery is solved. Some old guy has been sneaking around town ripping people off. Now he's on his way to jail. Case closed. And you've got terrific digital images of the whole shakedown. Good job, Alex. You're amazing!"

The boy turned back toward the window. "I don't know," he said quietly. "I just don't know."

Beyond the limp curtains he could see the dim outline of the trees and sidewalks, and the moonlit form of the statue rising from its pedestal in the middle of Benson Park.

* * *

Mr. Cho looked down at the young, earnest faces staring up at him. Each member of the assembled group wore the carefully pressed and skillfully arranged uniform of their beloved Pathfinder club, all adorned with scarves, sashes, pins, and badges. He smiled, enjoying the enthusiasm shining in each eager eye. "I must say," he said, glancing over at Alex who sat between Shane and Alicia on the front row, "little did I know that when our very own Honors Club began their quest for their photography badge, one among them would become famous."

All eyes turned to Alex, who shifted in his seat and cleared his throat quietly.

The club leader held up the latest edition of the *Cyprus Hill Messenger.* "Alex Timmons made the front page with his outstanding photographs of the Benson Park arrest. I think we should give our budding photojournalist a rousing cheer for his hard work."

The room erupted with applause and whistles as the twenty-three members of the Cyprus Hill Pathfinder Club shouted their approval. Alex stood hesitantly to his feet and waved shyly, looking extremely uncomfortable. Mr. Cho motioned for the boy to come to the front of the room and stand beside him as he clapped along with the rest.

As the tumult continued, Alex lifted his hand. "My friend Kobe Myers brought the equipment," he shouted, trying to be heard. "He taught me how to use it. It wasn't just me."

Mr. Cho motioned for the group to take their seats. "Listen up, club," he ordered. "Alex has something he wants to say."

When the room grew quiet, Alex cleared his throat. "Kobe and I were trying to get a picture of a squirrel, and I just happened to see the man in the park. It was an accident. No big deal."

"No big deal?" A Pathfinder chuckled. "You nailed the guy who's been ripping us off. My dad said the old man even had some of the stuff that was stolen right in his pocket. You got him red-handed, and Sheriff Curtain is going to lift the curfew beginning tonight. I don't know about anybody else, but I think that makes you a hero!"

Cheers erupted again as Alex shifted his weight from one foot to another. "No, wait," he called. "Wait a minute." He looked around at the flushed, shouting faces and felt hands patting him on the back and punching him good-naturedly on the arm. "Wait," he pressed, trying to be heard. "You don't understand. I . . . I don't think he's the thief. He's just an old man, that's all."

Mr. Cho leaned forward. "How's it feel to be a hero?" he asked.

"I'm *not* a hero," Alex shouted, his words lost in the happy tumult. "I just took a picture of an old man in a park. That's all I did."

No one heard him. Everyone in the room, everyone in town, was relieved that the dark shadow of fear that had settled over them had finally been lifted. They'd been afraid to walk the streets. Every time they'd glanced out their windows at night, they'd wondered if the criminal was, at that very moment, stalking their homes or their businesses. The realization that the bad guy had been caught and now resided safe and secure in Sheriff Curtain's jail filled them with a brand of relief nothing could alter. Their uncertainty and stomach-gnawing fear was gone. Case closed.

Later in the evening, after the cheering had died down and important club business was attended to, the Pathfinders shifted their focus from the reluctant photographer to their marching drills. In a few weeks, the club would be taking part in the town's annual Summer Festival, and Mr. Cho had created some new routines he wanted everyone to try. Photography and heroism would have to wait. For now, identifying their right foot from their left gripped the attention of every member of the club, including Alex Timmons.

But even as he marched stiffly to the steady *beat, beat, beat* of Shane's snare drum, the boy would occasionally glance at the darkened window at the far end of the church's recreation room. Out there was a sad, old man being held captive in a jail cell for a crime Alex believed he didn't commit. But, no one would listen to him. No one would believe him when he insisted that the man the police had nabbed wasn't the hardware store thief.

He wasn't exactly sure why he felt that way. Maybe it was the shocked look on the man's face when the police officers rushed him. Maybe it was the way he'd struggled as his hands were cuffed. Maybe it was the fear that was reflected in his face as they led him out of the park and shoved him into the waiting squad car. Bad guys know all about being arrested. They've probably experienced it before. This man looked totally unprepared for what happened to him that night.

Alex shook his head as if to clear his thoughts as he spun about and marched smartly beside his fellow Pathfinders, their carefully shined shoes stomping out the rhythm of the routine. The police officers did find a small pocketknife hidden in the old man's pants—the very same kind of knife that had been stolen from the store. And what about that new pair of work gloves found in his thin, worn jacket? They were on the hardware store's stolen list as well.

The boy frowned. Why would a stranger be carrying gloves in the middle of summer in a town park at three o'clock in the morning? Yes, there was plenty of evidence to connect him to the robbery. That's why Sheriff Curtain had felt confident enough to lift the curfew. But the old man simply didn't look or act like a thief. He just didn't!

Alex turned with the others in his line and gave a smart salute to Mr. Cho, who stood at attention at the head of the room. *Boom, boom, BOOM!* Shane's drum sounded the final beats of the routine as their leader grinned broadly. "Not bad," he called to the neat rows of Pathfinders standing stiffly before him. "Not bad at all! Let's do it just one more time before we go home."

As Alex and the others took up their first positions to begin the routine again, the boy glanced at the dark window, a fresh resolve driving his thoughts. Yes, he'd find the answers to his troubling questions. If the man in the park wasn't the thief, that meant that somewhere out there was a real crook who was probably having a good laugh over the photographs in the paper. Perhaps he was preparing another visit to the midnight streets of their sleeping town. However, this time maybe someone—someone just minding his or her own business—might get in his way. The boy shuttered when he remembered that the real thief carried something in his jacket that was a lot more dangerous than a small pocketknife and a pair of work gloves.

Chapter 5

Bandit in a Cage

Sheriff Curtain looked up from his desk as Alex tapped lightly on his office door. "Hey, young man," he called. "Come on in."

The boy selected a chair beside the file cabinet and waited for the officer to finish writing something on a pad of paper resting beside his computer.

"What brings you out on this warm summer evening?" the sheriff asked as he jammed his pen into the cup by his elbow. "Shane said you guys are doing marching drills at Pathfinders. How's it going?"

"Good," Alex responded. "Pretty good."

The man studied his visitor for a long moment and then sighed. "He's our guy, Alex," he said. "And, no, we haven't gotten a confession out of him yet. As a matter of fact, we can't even get him to tell us his name."

"Can I see him?"

"Alex."

"Please, Sheriff Curtain. I know I've been calling you for the last two days, and I know you keep telling me no, but, I just want to talk to him for a few minutes. I . . . I kinda feel like it's my fault he's in jail. Kobe and I saw him in the park. We called your deputies. And . . . I took all those stupid pictures."

The officer chuckled. "Those *stupid pictures* as you call them, brought a whole lot of relief to this town, Alex. People were scared to walk out their front door. Suddenly they see photographs printed in the newspaper of the bad guy getting caught. Folks are breathing again, thanks to you and Kobe."

"Then . . . can I see him?"

Sheriff Curtain lifted his hands in a gesture of reluctant consent. "OK, OK. Then maybe you'll leave my poor overworked and understaffed police department alone."

Alex stood. "It won't take long. I . . . I just want to ask him something."

The officer crossed the room and walked out into the hallway. "Your mother will probably have my hide for this, but I'll have one of my men take you downstairs."

The door hinges to the basement protested loudly as the uniformed deputy led the young visitor into the "Confinement Area," as the sign above the entry proclaimed. The walls of the large room were made of old, dusty brick, and the smell of wet soil hung in the air. The tile floor was swept clean and a collection of old, metal chairs guarded the far wall. In the center of the room rose a twelve-foot by twelve-foot cage-like enclosure lit by a single bulb hanging from the ceiling, its glaring glow tossing shadows in random patterns onto the walls.

"You've got a visitor," the officer called to the bulge under the cover of the single cot sitting at one side of the cell. "Treat him good. He's the only person in Cyprus Hill who says you're not our criminal."

The covers moved slightly. "He a lawyer?"

The deputy chuckled. "Nope. But, you might want to smile pretty. He's the fellow who took all of those really flattering pictures of you in the park." With that, the officer settled onto a nearby chair and began leafing through an outdated news magazine. "Go ahead," he called to Alex. "He's all yours."

The boy walked to the edge of the cell and cleared his throat. "Ah . . . hello, sir. I'm . . . I'm Alex Timmons."

He saw the covers slowly retreat, revealing an unshaven head and a deeply lined, tanned face. Dark, tired eyes stared at him from below a thatch of wayward, snow-white hair. "You're just a kid," the old man said.

"Yeah," Alex responded. "That's what my mom keeps telling me."

The prisoner sat up stiffly and lowered his feet to the floor. Alex noticed that his socks were stained and torn. "What do you wanna see me about? Planning on taking some more pictures for your criminal collection?"

"Oh, no." The boy hesitated. "Well, maybe later. You see, I'm getting my photography honor in Pathfinders and . . ."

"Pathfinders?"

Alex nodded. "It's at my church. Kinda like Boy Scouts except we talk about God and stuff."

The old man chuckled. "So, what were you doing taking pictures of me in the middle of the night with a light-enhancing digital camera?"

Alex gasped. "You know about photography?"

"I know a lot about a lot of things," the prisoner responded coldly. "And look where it got me." The two were silent for a moment. "What do you want to see me about?"

Alex glanced around the enclosure. "Are you . . . OK?"

The prisoner scratched himself. "Do I look OK?"

"No," the boy said hesitantly. "No, you don't. And I'm really sorry. I was just trying to get a picture of a squirrel."

The old man rose and shuffled to the bars, facing his visitor. "You got me confused with a squirrel?"

Alex smiled in spite of himself. "Oh, no, sir. I . . ." He cleared his throat. "I . . . just wanted to ask you something."

"What?"

The boy looked first one way then another and leaned close to the bars. "Did you do it? Did you rob the hardware store?"

The prisoner checked to his right and left, then leaned forward as well. "No," he said.

A sarcastic chuckle echoed from the direction of the folding chair at the far end of the room. "Well then," the deputy called, "we'd just better open these doors and let you out. Oh, wait, there's the matter of the stolen merchandise we found in your possession. And the fact that you were in town at three o'clock in the morning smack dab in the middle of a curfew." He tapped his forehead with the palm of his hand. "One more thing. Since we locked you up, there hasn't been another robbery attempt. Strange. Care to explain?"

The old man shook his head. "Why try? You've already convicted me. As for the stolen merchandise, I told you I found that stuff in the warehouse behind that . . . that big antique store near the filling station. The pocketknife and gloves were lying on the floor, so I just picked 'em up. How was I supposed to know they were stolen?"

The deputy laughed. "And you were sitting on a park bench at three o'clock in the morning completely by mistake, right? One moment you were at home with the grandchildren and then you suddenly woke up in the middle of Cyprus Hill. Give me a break, old man. Besides, if you're so innocent, why don't you give us your name?"

"You won't believe me if I tell you," the prisoner shot back.

Alex lifted his hand. "Sir, where in the warehouse did you find the pocketknife and gloves?"

"What?"

"Where did you find them? Downstairs, upstairs? In the backroom? On the loading dock?"

The old man studied the face of his young visitor. "Downstairs, by the back door." He hesitated. "Hey, kid. Why do you think I'm innocent when everyone else is ready to lock me up for life?"

Alex shook his head. "I don't know. Maybe . . . you just look like someone who wouldn't rob a hardware store. Besides . . ."

"Yes?"

"I . . . feel like I know you, like I've seen you somewhere before. Are you from around here?"

The old man sighed. "Listen kid, I appreciate your visit and your vote of confidence." He glanced at the deputy then back at the boy. "I'm not the Cyprus Hill Bandit as the newspaper says. I *am* innocent of what they said I did."

Alex nodded slowly. "Sir," he pressed, "why were you in the park so late at night?"

The prisoner walked back to his cot and sat down with a heavy sigh. "I was visiting a ghost," he said, almost in a whisper.

"That does it!" the deputy declared, jumping to his feet. "Alex, you'll have to go now. This guy is loony tunes, and you shouldn't be anywhere near him. Go home, now! Go."

Alex moved to the door and paused. He turned and glanced back at the prisoner, who sat gazing at him from behind the heavy bars. The old man looked lost, alone, like an animal trapped in a cage. "I believe you," he called. "I still believe you."

With that he turned and left the room.

* * *

The next day, dark clouds swept in from the west and began soaking the town with sheets of rain. Sharp, bright stabs of lightning and deep-throated thunder sent the citizens of Cyprus Hill running for cover. Roads and sidewalks became miniature rivers coursing past empty stores and dimly lit eateries. Those who did venture out into the storm hid under large umbrellas and splashed through puddles as they ran between whatever cover they could find.

The park was empty, except for the occasional tourist couple who thought that the rain only added to the romantic charm of the little West Virginia town.

Alex, Shane, and Alicia, never ones to waste a summer day even when the ducks were walking, sat on a park bench near the base of the statue, huddled under an oversized umbrella sporting a West Virginia Mountaineers logo, the state's college football team. The three sat in silence, watching rivulets of rain wash down the bronze face of the town hero, Harry Benson, who stood at his post, arm outstretched, pointing at the bank.

"Then what did he say?" Alicia asked.

"That he didn't do it."

"And you believe him?"

Alex sighed. "What are you supposed to do when everyone says one thing and you say another?"

Shane kicked at a puddle forming at his feet. "My dad says they're going to move him to the county jail in Hillbrook tomorrow. He said the state police want to ask him some questions too. This guy must've done a lot of bad stuff if everyone is so interested in him."

"Yeah, well," Alicia said, watching a giggling college couple hurry past, their umbrella turned inside-out by a gust of wind, "I know I'll feel even safer when he's in Hillbrook. Dad's jail might be OK for a few nights, but even he says it's not exactly escape-proof. If the Cyprus Hill Bandit put his mind to it, he could probably figure out a way of getting himself free, and then we'd be right back where we started."

Alex brushed moisture from his face and continued to stare up at the statue. "Even if he is who the newspaper says he is, I still feel sorry for him—locked up in a cage like a rabbit or coyote with no one to talk to. Besides, didn't Mr. Cho say we're supposed to love our enemies?"

Alicia laughed. "Well, I love the fact that the Cyprus Hill Bandit is in my dad's jail. Does that work?"

Shane nodded. "Works for me."

"You guys are depressing," Alex said with a chuckle. Then he sat in silence for a long moment. "I just wonder . . ."

"Wonder what?"

The boy stood up. "I'm going to go exploring. Wanna come?"

"Where?"

"I don't know; the woods by the college, down by the creek, the old warehouse?"

The siblings shook their heads. "Nah," Shane said, "you go ahead. Mom wants us home early for supper. Gonna make pizza with mushrooms and everything. My dad's favorite."

"Maybe I'll stop by later," Alex called as he headed down the sidewalk, rain splashing off his head and shoulders. "Save me a piece."

The group moved away, running through the puddles, leaving Harry Benson to face the storm alone.

By the time Alex reached the old warehouse at the edge of town, the rain had shifted from a downpour to a flood Noah might have recognized. The raindrops themselves had become larger and much colder, adding an uncomfortable sting as they hit the boy's bare skin. Their size and temperature indicated that they were falling from a greater height—something the three members of the Honors Club had learned while earning their weather badge.

The inside of the large, wooden building smelled like rotting timbers, which was probably one of the reasons why no business had used the structure for years. Everyone seemed perfectly happy just to let it grow old and crumble away. So, there it stood, waiting for the inevitable. Alex was happy the building remained where it stood for it provided him and his friends endless opportunities for exploring and imagining.

He walked along the darkened hallway leading to the loading dock and paused to stare out at the vast, empty expanse where a busy sock factory once operated. If he ignored the rumble of thunder and constant drumming of the rain, he could almost hear the repetitive rattle of machinery that years ago had stitched fabric into footwear.

On this particular evening, Alex wanted to do more than let his imagination give reason for every creak and groan of the old, sagging, two-story structure. He was on a mission, the cause for which he wasn't exactly sure. The old man had mentioned that he'd found the pocketknife and gloves on the first floor, and Alex figured he'd see if there might be more evidence hiding among the shadows.

He began by exploring the second floor, which had once housed the factory and warehouse offices. All that remained were piles of discarded papers, mostly black-and-white sales brochures declaring in no uncertain terms that "Cyprus Hill socks feel good, wear good, and last almost forever." Newspapers sporting advertisements from businesses the boy had never heard of lay scattered about, left by previous visitors and, more than likely, overnight occupants of the abandoned building.

The loading docks faced the woods at the rear of the structure, their cement and wooden ramps ending abruptly where trucks once waited to accept endless streams of boxes coming from the packaging and shipping departments. Even now, the smell of burnt diesel fuel and machine oil lingered in the damp air, the odor absorbed by the wooden rafters and block walls holding up the weatherworn roof angling overhead.

Next, Alex wandered into the factory area itself, a dark empty space floored with wood and surrounded by walls that had once kept the cold and wind off the shoulders of the workers. Now, most of the insulation was gone, leaving only the skeletal remains of timber and plywood, copper wiring, and twisted radiator pipes.

The boy pulled his arms into his chest as a cold wind, pushed down by the storm, whistled through the rough openings in the walls and made the structure moan like a dying animal. There was nothing new to see, just empty space and a few packing boxes that had, for years, served as home sweet home to the old factory's growing population of rodents.

Clunk. A noise echoed down the corridors at the back of the building and rattled the broken glass of the window by his head. Alex jumped, startled by the sudden sound.

Clunk, bump. This time the noise was closer.

Alex moved out onto the loading dock and looked around, feeling suddenly exposed and very uncomfortable. "Is . . . is someone there?" he called, hoping against hope that there'd be no answer. He fully understood that buildings, especially old ones caught in the grip of summer storms, made noises. But this wasn't a simple rattle or throaty moan. It was . . .

Bump, bump, clunk. OK. This wasn't fun anymore. Something, or some*one,* was moving about above his head on the second floor. The boy hurried back into the factory and started making his way as quickly and as quietly as possible toward the distant hallway that led to the front entrance. Whoever or whatever wanted this building could have it. He'd be happy to leave it in their care.

Bump, bump, CRASH! The sound of shattering glass added just the incentive Alex needed to break into a run. He raced across the empty expanse, skidded around the corner, and entered the hallway at full speed. He could see the front entrance up ahead, appearing and disappearing as lightning flickered through the openings in the wall and spilled through the broken, dust-stained windows overhead.

At that moment, his foot contacted something hard, and the boy fell forward, carried by the momentum of his frantic escape. His chest and face slammed hard onto the floor, and his body swept forward, skidding across the dirty surface like a baseball player sliding toward home plate.

Suddenly, his forward motion stopped as he rammed into something heavy and unmoving. "Oh!" he cried out as he felt his shoulders bend and his legs jam into his chest. Then all was quiet, save for the steady drone of the rain and insistent rumble of thunder.

In the semi-darkness, Alex opened his eyes to find that his head was pressing against a pair of muddy boots. Looking up, he saw the form of a man standing over him, an iron rod held tightly in his hands. As lightning flashed outside, fingers of brilliant illumination filtered through the window and touched the face looming overhead. Dark eyes stared at him as drops of water tumbled from broad shoulders. "No!" Alex gasped as he fought the almost uncontrollable urge to scream. "No!"

Chapter 6

Potty Break

The phone rang in Sheriff Curtain's kitchen just as the man filled his mouth with pizza. "I'm eating supper!" he declared into the handset, the words muffled by a mixture of tomato sauce, mushrooms, and warm dough.

Alicia and Shane glanced over at their father just as he slammed the phone back onto its cradle. "Telemarketers again?" Mrs. Curtain called from the table.

The man didn't answer. Instead he hurried to the kitchen door and took down his holstered gun from a shelf high above the refrigerator. "Stay inside," he commanded, pointing his finger at his family in a firm, no-questions-asked gesture.

A second later, he was gone.

Shane and Alicia ran to the window and saw that their father was already in his squad car. With a roar, the engine sprang to life, the vehicle backed down the driveway toward the street, and then, in a cloud of burning rubber, sped away.

Deputy Sam Pester was just exiting the Confinement Area when his boss clattered down the stairs two at a time, almost knocking him down. "Where?" the sheriff shouted.

"In the bathroom. I thought he'd been in there for a little longer than usual. When I went to check, he was gone."

The two hurried to the small enclosure fronting the basement and Sheriff Curtain threw open the door. The bars that had covered the small window near the ceiling lay by the toilet. Broken glass littered the floor.

"And you didn't hear him?" the sheriff gasped.

Sam shook his head. "He musta broken the window during a thunder hit," he responded defensively. "It's raining, you know. I searched the building and even questioned people out on the street. No one saw nothin'."

"And the reason you didn't call me as soon as you found out he was gone was . . .?"

"You were home eating supper. And I know how much you like pizza, especially with mushrooms. Personally, I prefer olives and . . ."

"Call Frank and Terry. Call everyone! Thanks to you, we've got an escaped criminal on the loose."

The deputy followed his boss out of the basement and up the stairs. "Hey, I didn't just let him go. He broke out of a jail bathroom that I don't mind saying isn't the most secure in the world. Even though he's an old man, he tore those bars out of the window like they were held in place by chewing gum."

Sheriff Curtain spun around. "I don't care if the building fell down around him, he was your responsibility and you blew it!"

"I'm sorry, I'm sorry. What more can I say?"

The officer softened. "Look Sam, I know it's not your fault, and I know our jail is a joke. But we were going to move him out of here tomorrow morning. You should have guarded him more closely."

The deputy lifted his hand. "Hold on a minute," he said. "I'll gladly chase down speeders and track bad guys through the desert. I'll even stake out serial killers and wrestle pickpockets on the street. But I draw the line at watching a prisoner . . ."

"OK, OK," Sheriff Curtain interrupted with a chuckle. "You've made your point. Just get the team together and let's find our man. He didn't have any car keys on him when he was arrested, so we can assume he's on foot. As soon as the other deputies get here, start going door-to-door. Check everywhere—stores, alleyways, the park, behind the antique shop, the warehouse—everywhere. I'm calling the mayor and then Mr. Shepherd to see if we can figure out how to keep the good people of Cypress Hill from going into a full-fledged panic. Now get going!"

The two men headed for their phones as outside the thunder rolled and a cold rain continued to pour.

* * *

Alex squirmed as rough coils of rope chaffed his wrists. Across the darkened room, the old man stood at a broken window watching the downpour, his face stern and expressionless. Snow-white hair lay in wet, twisted strands over his ears and forehead.

"Why'd you tie me up?" the boy called, feeling more anger than fear.

"So you wouldn't run and tell the sheriff and his hot-shot deputy where I was." He turned. "Don't worry, I'm not going to hurt you. I just need time to think."

"Can you think without me being tied up?" Alex asked with a frustrated sigh. "I won't go anywhere and tell anybody anything. Besides, you've got these ropes too tight. My hands are all tingly."

The old man's shoulders sagged. "I'm not a bad person. I'm really not."

Alex twisted in his chair. "Well, it's kinda hard for me to tell since you're keeping me as prisoner in this old warehouse and you won't let any circulation get to my fingers."

The stranger crossed the room and stood before the boy. "Do you promise not to leave?"

"Yes. Please untie me. Please."

The old man nodded. "All right. But I'm going to hold you to your word. Sometimes that's all a man's got. His word. Without it, he's nothing."

As soon as his hands were free, Alex rubbed his wrists and shook his fingers, trying to revive feeling in them. The old man watched for a moment, then returned to the window. Beyond the shattered glass, the lights of Cyprus Hill shimmered in the storm, revealing dark, wet streets and wind-blown trees.

"So," Alex called as he continued messaging his hands, "why'd you escape? Why'd you run away from Sheriff Curtain's jail?"

"You sure ask a lot of questions."

"Yeah. That's what my mom says."

Alex heard his companion chuckle. "I guess that's OK, asking questions. Good way to learn." The old man paused. "I ran away because that's what I do. I'm good at it. I've had plenty of practice."

"You've escaped out of jails before?"

"No. This was a first."

Alex frowned. "I don't understand. If you're innocent, why run?"

The old man turned. "Sometimes it's not what you are that matters," he said, lowering himself to the floor and resting his forehead against his knees. "It's what people think you are. You can be as innocent as a newborn baby, but if someone thinks you're bad, you're bad. Works the other way around too."

Alex thought for a moment. "My mom says I shouldn't care what people think. I should just be a good person and always do the best I can."

The old man nodded. "Your mom's smart." Then he hesitated, searching for words. "Sometimes people think you're good when you're not. They might even get to calling you a hero and you know you're nothing but a coward." He raised his head and faced his young companion. "That's when things can get confusing."

Alex sat in silence, trying to comprehend what the stranger was saying. He was right, in a way. The boy knew that the old man wasn't the Cypress Hill Bandit. But, the whole town, including the sheriff, thought otherwise. That's why he was in jail.

And the part about being a hero made sense too. Hadn't the entire Pathfinder club called him that even though he knew all he'd done was shoot a picture of a sad, old man sitting by a statue?

Alex stared at the wet, deeply lined face sitting across from him. He studied the raindrops dripping from the white hair and watched them flow slowly down the cheek, nose, and mouth of his strange companion.

The boy blinked. The curve of the cheek, the tilt of the nose, the shape of the mouth, they all looked strangely familiar, as if he'd seen them before, not once, but many times. Alex frowned. It was a feeling he'd been struggling with for days, ever since he'd taken the pictures of the arrest.

He closed his eyes, replaying images from his past, faces he'd seen in photographs, relatives, school friends, men he'd met in the stores and restaurants lining Mercer Street. Then he placed himself in the park and, in his mind's eye, looked up at the statue.

The thought almost took his breath away.

In an instant Alex was on his feet, staring wide-eyed at the man resting against the far wall of the dark, damp room. "You . . . you . . . you're the statue. You're . . . Harry Benson," he gasped.

The old man lifted his face and sat staring at his companion. His eyes reflected an unspeakable hurt, a hidden agony. "Harry Benson died in Korea. He died a hero."

"No he didn't," Alex countered, amazed that he was saying what he was saying. "You're him. You're the statue in Benson Park."

The boy heard the old man sigh, the sound almost a groan. "I'm not the hero they think I am," he said. "I didn't save those men because I was noble or brave. I was running away, trying to escape the bullets and the bombs." His words became heavy with emotion. "Some of the men saw me and asked me what I was doing. I told them that I'd found a safe passage back to Seoul, and they believed me. I didn't know where I was going! I just wanted to get away, to save my own skin. When I looked back, they were following me, like I was their leader or something! The whole platoon fell in behind me, and we stumbled along for miles, walking past the dead and dying, picking our way through the incredible litter of war. It was luck. That's all. Dumb luck. We could have gotten ourselves killed. Those men could have followed me to their death!"

Alex stood unmoving, listening to the cries of a man who, for decades, had carried the awful truth about an event Cypress Hill had celebrated for as long as he could remember.

"I tossed my dog tags when we got back behind friendly lines," the old man continued. "Then I just faded into the countryside, running, running, putting as much distance between me and the war as I could. I eventually smuggled myself out of the country on a freighter and spent the next thirty years moving from island to island; Singapore, the Philippines, Indonesia, Japan, anywhere I could live my life without facing the truth. I assumed a new identity and when I felt enough time had passed that the military couldn't prosecute me as a deserter, I returned to the United States. Came here to Cypress Hill, the town in which I was born. And what did I see? A statue of me saying I was a war hero, a brave, fearless soldier who saved people and gave his life for his country.

"Over the past few years, I've come back to town from time to time, always late at night, to sit and think. The statue reminds me of what I should have been, what I *could* have been."

The old man turned to face Alex. "Listen to me, kid. Lies can be powerful. They can hide the truth under a very comfortable blanket of fantasy. But lies have a way of destroying you from the inside out, eating away at you like a cancer. They're dangerous. Very dangerous."

Alex walked over to the man and sat down beside him. He didn't know what to say, how to relate to the real-life version of someone he'd admired for so many years. The face on the statue was young, determined, full of life. The face of the old man, although shaped by the very same features, was more than old. It appeared tired, hopeless, with no inner spark of life. It was as if the strength of the statue had drained away, leaving a weatherworn, empty shell. "So," the boy said softly, "what are you going to do?"

His companion sighed, wiping moisture from his face with a trembling hand. "I don't know. I've heard people say that the statue helped their children want to be heroes when they grew up. I've heard men say that they were inspired by what Private Harry Benson did, how it helped them face tough situations in their lives. If I tell the truth, what will happen to all those people? What will happen to their self-confidence and sense of pride? What will happen to this town if they lose their hero?"

* * *

Sheriff Curtain shone his flashlight down the dark alley and squinted through the rain. He was tired and hungry. His single bite of pizza had long ago lost whatever energy it promised to provide.

He was also angry. Being the sheriff in a small town carried with it a lot of responsibility. People looked up to him, counted on him for protection from the harmful elements that stalked every pocket of civilization. And, like in most out-of-the-way towns, the budget for law enforcement was small, barely enough to meet payroll and keep gas in the patrol cars. Even the computer resting on the desk in his office was old, struggling to run the newer programs designed to make his work more efficient.

Now, here he was, slogging through a downpour, trying to recapture an old man who'd found a way to exit the department's Confinement Area without permission. No, it wasn't Sam's fault. It was the result of tiny budgets, aging facilities, and an obliging storm.

"Anything?" he called to his deputy at the far end of the alley.

"Nope. Just an empty beer can and a very wet cat."

Curtain chuckled. "OK. Come on. Let's try the next block. Maybe Terry or Frank are having better luck."

Sam emerged from the shadows and joined his boss as the two walked along the deserted sidewalk, seeking temporary shelter under awnings and glowing store signs. "So, who do you think this guy is?" the deputy asked, shining his light into the candy store window near the corner. "Even his fingerprints weren't on record in Charleston. He had no wallet, no ID. It's like he doesn't exist."

Sheriff Curtain shrugged under his shimmering raincoat. "Beats me. Probably just a drifter. His mode of operation matches a thousand guys in our state. They blow into a town, steal stuff, and pawn them off in the next city for cash before moving on and doing it all over again. Some way to live, huh?"

"What about the gun?" the deputy pressed. "The first picture that Timmons kid took showed a guy holding a gun. Where do you suppose the weapon is now?"

The sheriff shook his head. "Maybe he hid it somewhere so he wouldn't be caught with it on him. It's probably unregistered or stolen. I'm sure he knows exactly where that weapon is and will be going back to get it. One thing's for certain; an old man is just an old man, but an old man with a gun can be dangerous."

Sam nodded. "I just hope he has enough sense not to use it. The idea that somewhere out here is an unstable senior citizen packing a revolver is enough to make you lose sleep at night."

"Tell me about it," the sheriff stated.

The two turned the corner and headed down the street, their flashlights tossing sharp beams into the storm as their brilliance pierced the sodden shadows. Both men would rather have been at home with their families, enjoying the warmth and dryness of their dens. But there was a job to do. Police officers didn't become police officers to be comfortable. They took on the responsibility willingly, choosing summer storms and late-night searches over the lure of home and safety in order to keep the peace. It was a noble calling. On this particular night, it was a very wet calling as well.

* * *

The old man lifted his hand and placed his finger over his lips. Alex saw him rise slowly and make his way across the room, tiptoeing as he went.

"What's th . . ."

Benson jabbed his finger to his lips again, shutting off his companion's question in mid-word.

The boy listened. All he could hear was the drumming of the rain and distant rattle of thunder. "Someone's coming," the man reported, his mouth forming the words without making a sound.

Alex strained to hear. Yes. He could just make out the slow *tap, tap, ta-tap* of footsteps echoing from behind the closed door. They were random, hesitant, as if someone was looking for something in the large factory area beyond the wall.

The boy knew who'd be out there. Sheriff Curtain's reputation of tracking down bad guys was well known throughout the county. Just last year, he'd cornered a criminal in the woods in back of the college. The guy was wanted in four states for, among other things, putting his wife in the hospital during a domestic dispute. The sheriff had cornered him in a ravine and managed to bring him to justice single-handedly.

The footsteps grew nearer. Alex saw the look of panic that had spread across his companion's face slowly melt into a calm resolve. The old man's race from the truth was about to end. He knew that Sheriff Curtain would eventually discover Benson's true identity one way or another. All he'd really have to do is stand and stare at him long enough to make the connection to the much-admired face in the park.

The man glanced over at Alex. "I'm sorry, kid," he said in a whisper. "I'm sorry I got you into this."

The footsteps paused as the knob on the door leading into the room turned one way, then another. With a *click,* the portal began to open. The hinges voiced their age and lack of lubricant as the old, dusty door swung inward and a looming figure entered the room. Suddenly, lightning flashed across the sky and lit up the darkness with a staccato brilliance. In that instant, the new arrival saw that he wasn't alone. Also in that instant, Alex and his companion recognized that the stranger wasn't Sheriff Curtain or any of his deputies.

A gun appeared from the man's jacket and a rough, angry voice called out, "Don't move. Don't move a hair or I'll shoot you both dead!"

Chapter 7

Running Away

"Well, well, what have we here?" The stranger stood in the doorway, dark eyes squinting into the shadows, mouth twisted into a mocking grin. "An old man and a kid. Is it story time in the ol' warehouse?" He sat down on a large cardboard box by the door. "Tellin' the young'n about the good ol' days, Grandpa? Or is someone having a birthday party? Hey, yeah, let's have a party. Just us and the rats. How 'bout it?"

The man, who appeared to be in his mid-thirties, looked as if he hadn't shaved for a week. His rain-soaked jacket hung from narrow shoulders, and the baseball cap he wore low over his ears did little to contain the strands of matted, dark brown hair jutting from his head in odd angles.

"Who are you?" the old man asked, eyeing the stranger from across the room.

"Me? Oh, I'm just a guy passin' through. Stopped by to collect my treasures." He patted the

box under his legs. "You can't have too many treasures you know. The local hardware store was kind
enough to have a sale just for me a little while
back. Everything I could carry absolutely free! Well
I'm here to tell you that I can carry a *lot* of stuff,
especially when the price is right."

Alex gasped. "I know who you are. You're the
Cypress Hill Bandit!"

The stranger laughed, his rough, crackling
voice revealing a long relationship with ciga-
rettes. "Hey, I read about that in the newspaper," he said. "Must say, I'm flattered. I ain't
never had a fancy name given to me before.
Course, a couple days later I noticed that the
police nailed the wrong guy in your silly park.
Jumped him in the middle of the night. So right
now he's sittin' in jail while I . . ." The man stiffened. "Wait a minute." He slowly walked across
the room, his hand adjusting its grip on the
weapon. "Hey, ain't you the old geezer they arrested? Yeah. You're him, all right. White hair.
Big nose. Saw your picture in the paper. In one
of the shots, you had two deputies kneeling on
your chest. That had to hurt."

"What do you want?" the old man asked.

"Like I said, I've come for my stuff."

"What stuff?"

The stranger lifted his hands. "What are you,
dense? The treasures I got at the hardware store!

Tools, ammo, fishing gear, work clothes, stuff like that. I even borrowed a wheelbarrow so I could carry it all. Got as far as this warehouse and decided I should take only what I could run with and come back later for the rest, you know, after the excitement of my visit died down a bit. Then I read that they'd caught the Cypress Hill Bandit so, here I am! I stashed some of the loot right here in this handy box." He paused. "Have you seen the prices of hardware goods lately? It's criminal what they charge. What's a law-abiding fellow like me to do?"

"Law abiding hardly describes you," the old man shot back.

"Well, actually, that hardly describes *you*, my aged friend. They think *you* broke into the store. Which brings me to the obvious. What're you doin' out of jail? I thought they had you all tucked away in the sheriff's office. What'd you do, bribe the guard? Someone slip you a file in an apple pie?" The stranger pointed at Alex. "And you, young man, who are you and what are you doin' here with this dangerous, escaped prisoner? You two related or somethin'?"

The boy shook his head. "No."

The stranger's mood darkened. "All I know is I gotta think about this situation for a minute. I mean, I can't have you two runnin' around town knowing who I am."

"What are you planning on doing with us?" the old man asked, moving a little closer to Alex.

"Maybe I'll just shoot you!" the stranger teased. "Bang, bang. Problem solved."

Alex's older companion frowned. "Not a good idea."

"Why?"

"Then you'll be a thief and a murderer. The law doesn't look kindly on thieving, and they get *really* upset when it comes to people shooting each other."

The stranger lifted his hands. "Yeah, yeah, yeah. I know. Could affect my retirement plans. A famous bandit like me can't be too careful."

"Maybe you could let us go," Alex interjected, his heart pounding. "We promise not to tell anyone about you."

"Oh, sure. That's going to happen." The stranger laughed. "I just let you walk out of here and you go straight to the sheriff and say, 'Hey Sheriff, how are you tonight? Oh, by the way, there's some guy with a gun out at the warehouse gettin' the stuff he stole from the hardware store. But, remember, you didn't hear it from us." The man glared at Alex. "Do you think I'm stupid?"

"No, sir," the boy whispered.

The stranger smiled. "No, *sir.* I like that. Kid shows respect for his elders."

"Which is a lot more than you do," the old man stated coldly.

The bandit and glared at his older companion. "You got a death wish or something, Grandpa?"

"Look," the old man continued. "Why don't you let me go? You said yourself that I'm a wanted man. Do you think *I'm* going to run up to the first cop I see? Fat chance! They'd dump me right back in jail and toss away the key. I got news for you. I don't like being in jail. I don't like it at all."

Alex's mouth dropped open as he drew in a sharp breath.

"Just let me go and you'll have one less problem to worry about. I get away. You get away. And the kid? Hey, he's just a boy. No one will believe what he says about you. They'll think he's just making up a story to get attention. You know how kids are today. They live in a make-believe world filled with make-believe heroes and villains. No one listens to 'em."

The boy gasped. "What are you doing?"

"So, we got a deal?"

The stranger narrowed his eyes. "You know, for an old geezer, you sure are one cold dude. You're willing to leave this kid with me so you can save your own hide?"

"We got a deal or what?" the old man pressed. "I walk. You get your stuff."

"Fine with me," the stranger said with a chuckle.

"No!" Alex shouted. "Wait, you can't leave me here! What do you think you're doing?"

The old man turned to face the boy. "I'm doing what I do best," he said. "I'm running away."

With that he walked across the room. Alex saw him pause at the door and look back in his direction. "Remember, kid," he called, "sometimes it's what people think about you that's important." Then he was gone.

The bandit shook his head. "Now that's a coward if I ever saw one."

Alex nodded, fear tightening his throat. "Yeah. I guess he is."

"Well then," the man said turning to face his companion. "The only question that remains is, What am I going to do with you?"

Lightning shimmered beyond the walls of the warehouse, illuminating the face of the bandit. Alex's heart skipped a beat when he noticed that his face wore a wide, evil grin.

* * *

Rose Timmons was exiting the front door of her house when Sheriff Curtain arrived. The woman looked worried as she hurried toward the patrol car. "He didn't come home for supper," the officer heard her say as she slipped into the back seat behind Sam. "I've called all his friends. No one has seen or heard from him. Sheriff, it's not like him to stay out so late, especially in a storm."

Curtain put his cruiser in gear. "I don't mean to frighten you unduly, Rose," he said, "but we have another situation that may nor may not be connected to Alex."

"What do you mean?"

"Well, you know the man we're holding for the hardware store break-in?"

"The Cypress Hill Bandit?"

"Yes."

"What does he have to do with my son?"

The sheriff guided his car down the dark, rain-swept street. "I . . . I kinda let Alex and him meet with each other earlier today."

"You what?"

"Alex wore me down, Rose. He called again and again and, well, I finally said it was OK. My deputy was in the room for the whole visit."

"You let my little boy talk to a captured criminal in your jail cell? What on earth did you hope to accomplish?"

"Look, we don't know who this guy is and . . . well . . . I thought maybe he'd open up to Alex, maybe tell him his name or reveal something about his past. It was a long shot, I know. Besides, your son can be very persistent."

The woman leaned back in her seat. "You should have asked me first."

"I'm sorry, Rose. I really am. But, when I got your message that Alex was missing, I thought maybe the two events might be connected somehow and we should check with you before proceeding."

Rose frowned. "What two events?"

Sam turned in his seat. "The old man escaped."

"What?"

Sheriff Curtain glared at his deputy. "It seems that our prisoner got himself out of jail late this afternoon, right around supper time. Went out through the bathroom window."

"And you think my son is involved?" the woman gasped.

"No, no, not . . . involved. But, maybe he knows something. Maybe the old man told him what he was planning to do . . . passed him a note during their visit or something."

Rose shook her head. "Why in heaven's name would my child help a thief escape from jail? He doesn't even know who the man is!"

"Now, don't get upset," the sheriff stated, trying to calm his agitated passenger. "Alex told me that he felt kinda responsible for the old guy getting arrested and maybe, just maybe, he wanted to do something to help him out. Rose, your son is eleven years old. Kids that age can come up with some strange ideas. He may have felt guilty and wanted to stop feeling that way, so he agreed to help the guy get out of town by, I don't know, bringing him some food or a map."

Rose crossed her arms over her chest as frustrated tears spilled from her eyes. "Sheriff Curtain, you've misread my son. He's not a lawbreaker, and he certainly wouldn't help someone escape from justice even though he was involved in that person's capture."

"Then where is he, Rose? Where's Alex?"

"I don't know! But just because he's missing doesn't mean he's helping a criminal run away. He . . . might have fallen in the woods, got caught in the storm somewhere, or . . . or is hiding out in the old warehouse until the rain eases up. I just want to find him and know he's all right."

The sheriff blinked. "What did you say?"

"I want to know that . . ."

"No, before that."

Rose frowned. "I said he might be hiding in the old warehouse until the rain eases up."

Curtain grabbed his radio microphone. "Terry? Frank?"

Rose heard static, and then, "Yeah, Sheriff?"

"Frank, you checked the warehouse behind the antique shop, right?"

"Negative."

"Terry, how 'bout you?"

Static. Then, "I was going to stop by there on my next swing through the north side."

At that moment, the occupants of the patrol car saw a man running through the rain a block away, stumbling down the middle of the street, arms waving frantically. He looked totally out of breath, splashing through mud puddles and trying hard to keep upright as he battled the wind-driven downpour.

"Who's that?" Rose called.

Sheriff Curtain spun the wheel of his cruiser, causing the vehicle to skid sideways. The moment it stopped, he was out of the car, kneeling behind the hood, gun held out in front of him. "Stop!" He called. "Stop right now and drop to the ground."

The running man ignored the order and kept coming. "Help him," they heard him shout, his words breathless and choked. "You've got to help Alex!"

Rose's face turned ashen. "Alex! He said Alex!"

Sam joined his boss behind the car, weapon drawn. "What is he, crazy?"

"Get down on the ground NOW, old man!" the sheriff commanded, his revolver aimed dead center at the man's body.

The runner stumbled to a halt and stood, arms raised, chest heaving. "The warehouse," he said as he panted. "They're at the warehouse!"

"Who's at the warehouse?" Sheriff Curtain called.

"Alex, and a man with a gun. Help him. You've got to help Alex."

Curtain reached into the car and grabbed his radio. "All stations, converge on the warehouse on Liberty Street. Proceed with extreme caution. We've got an armed man and possibly a hostage. Keep it quiet, guys. We don't want to spook anybody. If you get there before I do, wait for me. Don't try anything heroic. This is a dangerous situation. I repeat, a *dangerous* situation."

Before the sheriff or his deputy could react, the old man raced to the car and climbed into the back seat. "Well, come on," he shouted through his labored breathing. "What are you waiting for? Let's go, let's go, let's GO!"

Curtain hesitated, then climbed in behind the wheel. Sam hurried to the passenger side and jumped in just as the cruiser sped off into the storm.

As the vehicle careened around the first corner, Rose glanced over at her unexpected companion. "Did you see Alex?"

"Yes."

"Was he OK?"

"He was when I left."

Rose studied the man's wet, fear-lined face.

"Why did you leave my son alone with a man who has a gun?"

Her companion didn't answer.

* * *

Alex watched as the bandit transferred items from the box into a large, worn mailbag he'd found elsewhere in the building. Work gloves, boxes of ammunition, hand tools, a rechargeable electric drill, band-saw blades, a small collection of diamond-tipped drill bits, and a rifle scope disappeared into the pouch accompanied by a running commentary from the thief.

"I'll bet you think I'm a bad person, right?"

"You're not?"

"Well, I didn't used to be. But I got kinda unhappy with the way my life was goin'. I had to work hard for everything. No one gave me nothin'. So, one day I says to myself, 'Self, why you workin' so hard? Take it easy. Live a little. Let other people work themselves to death in offices and factories. You? You just live off the land, you know, kinda like a farmer.' "

Alex frowned. "Farmers around here work very hard."

"OK. Maybe farmer isn't the right illustration. Anyway, I decided that insurance companies replace everything I rip off, so no one gets hurt and I get what I want. I can get a little cash and some nice power tools. It's a win-win situation for every-one."

The boy shook his head. "My mom says that when people steal, stores have to charge higher prices for stuff to help pay for insurance so everything costs more. Besides, none of those things belong to you. They're not yours so you shouldn't be taking them."

The bandit's expression changed to an angry scowl. "Hey kid, you just keep your mouth shut while I work. I can't stand your yap, yap, yapping all the time. Just sit over there and be quiet."

"Sorry."

"Yeah, well, you talk too much."

Alex sighed. "That's what my mom tells me too."

The boy was silent for a long moment. Then he suddenly called over to his companion. "Hey. That's a camera."

"Where?"

"There, in your hands. It's a brand new Mura digital camera, you know, one of those point-and-shoot kinds. I remember seeing it at the store. Mr. Zane showed it to me. It's totally awesome."

The bandit examined the box. "Is that what that is? I thought it was a depth finder, you know, for fishing."

"No. It's a digital camera. May . . . may I see it?"

The man tossed the carton in Alex's direction. "Knock yourself out, kid. It's no use to me. I don't know how to shoot pictures."

The boy lifted the device out of its box and turned it over slowly in his hands. "This is a really cool camera." He glanced over at his companion. "Want me to take your picture?"

The bandit laughed. "There ain't no film in that. Everyone knows you got to have film in a camera to shoot a picture. I'm not that stupid!"

Alex nodded. "Well, we could pretend. Yeah, I'll just snap a *pretend* picture of you. I mean, it's not everyday that a kid like me gets to photograph the real Cypress Hill Bandit."

The man's chin lifted slightly. "I am kind of a celebrity, ain't I?"

"Yeah. So, can I take your picture, even though there's no film in here?"

"Isn't it kinda dark?"

Alex pressed a button and a tiny flash flipped up over the lens. "No problem. I'll just use this!" Then the boy frowned. "Oh, except I don't have any batteries. Can't take a pretend picture without a battery."

"What size?" the bandit asked, rummaging through his bag.

"Double A," Alex called, opening the back of the camera. "Two of 'em."

"Here you go!" the bandit said, tossing the requested power supplies over to his young companion. "But make it snappy. I can't sit around here all night as you play photographer. I've got miles to put between me and this town before morning."

"OK," Alex said, slipping the batteries into place and pressing the camera's ON button. A second later, a green light shone at the top of the device, indicating it was ready to fire.

"Hey, it's got a timer and everything," the boy called. "Would you . . . would you mind if I get in the shot as well?"

The man sighed. "Just take the stupid picture. And be quick about it. I can't play games with you all night."

Alex set the camera on top of a nearby table and aimed it toward the bandit. Then he pressed the shutter. The green light began to blink. "Get ready," he said as he hurried over and stood beside the man. "And smile!"

For an instant, the room was illuminated by a bright flash as an almost inaudible *click* sounded from atop the table. Then everything was dark again, save for the occasional shimmer of lightning. "You happy now?" the man asked.

Alex ran to the camera and checked the settings. "I know one thing," he said, "it would have been a terrific picture, if we had film, of course."

"Sorry, kid," the bandit stated. "The last thing I want is my face plastered up all over the county. With my record, they'd toss me into jail in a second, and I'd be in there for a very long time."

"Don't worry," Alex responded. "You know us kids. Tons of imagination."

Suddenly, the two heard the sound of running feet coming from the factory. The bandit dropped his bag and turned to face the door, gun poised in front of him. Alex moved back against the wall, the camera held tightly in his hands. As the pounding footsteps grew louder, he cringed. Something bad was about to take place, and he knew he was going to be right in the middle of it.

The door burst open and, at that instant, two things happened. The bandit fired his gun, and Alex's finger, responding to the roar of the revolver, pressed down on the shutter of the little camera.

Chapter 8

Hero

"I don't believe it. I DON'T BELIEVE IT!"

Sheriff Curtain threw his raincoat over the chair in his office as he, Sam, Rose, and Alex entered the room. "We had him right in the palm of our hands. Right here." The man jabbed his finger into his open hand. "Then ol' Wild Bill Whoever-he-is sneaks away from us as we're planning our attack and runs into the warehouse like a narcotics agent on a drug raid. The perp gets off one shot and then vanishes," the man paused, "or at least that's what you say happened." The sheriff glared at Alex. "How do I know that you and the old man didn't just make up that story in order to cover the fact that the real Cypress Hill Bandit was the very same guy who busted out of my jail?"

"Sheriff Curtain!" Rose gasped. "Are you calling my son a liar?"

The officer's eyes narrowed. "All I know is that

when my deputies and I got to the room, we found the old guy and Alex surrounded by a lot of stolen merchandise. You do the math."

The woman stomped her foot on the floor. "That's not fair! Alex had nothing to do with the hardware store robbery. And why would the old man come running to find us just to lead us back to where he'd stored the stolen goods? The whole thing doesn't make sense and you know it!"

Sheriff Curtain lifted his hands. "Then where's the robber? Huh? Where's the bad guy? He wasn't in the room. All we found were Alex and the old codger. No one else!"

"Sir," Alex called hesitantly.

"You keep still, young man," the officer warned. "You're in a lot of trouble. A *lot* of trouble!"

Rose groaned in frustration. "This is ridiculous. Totally ridiculous! You're accusing my son of being involved in something he knew nothing about."

"Then where is this 'other' Cypress Hill Bandit? If he's not the old man, who is it?"

Alex stepped forward. "Sir, I really need to show you something."

"You keep quiet!"

"But, Sheriff."

The man lifted his finger and pointed at Alex.

"Don't say a word. Not another word!" Turning to the woman he added, "And you'd better get your son a good lawyer. This is more than you can handle alone."

As Rose and the sheriff continued to argue, Alex walked over to the man's desk where the station computer sat humming quietly, its screen littered with program icons.

"My son is not an accomplice to a robbery," the woman shouted. "He was home in bed when that hardware store was robbed, and the only reason he came to see the old man was because he felt guilty that he was partly responsible for getting him arrested. That's all there is to it. If you think that he and your escaped prisoner were somehow in cahoots with each other, you're totally insane."

The officer waved his arms in the air. "All I know is that there were only two people in that room in the warehouse. Only two. Alex and the old man. All around them, scattered like the leaves of autumn, was a thousand dollars worth of merchandise taken during the robbery. I know you love your son, and I know he's my children's best friend, but what I saw was what I saw. If there was a third person, the so-called *real* Cypress Hill Bandit in that room, where was he? Huh? Where was he when my deputies and I got there?"

"Sheriff Curtain," Alex called hesitantly.

"WHAT!"

"I think you need to see this."

"Alex, I'm finished talking to you. All you've done is tell me some cock-and-bull story about a mystical man with a gun who said he robbed the hardware store and that the old geezer went out to find help. That just doesn't cut it. If there was a third man in that warehouse, then SHOW HIM TO ME! You got that? Let me see the real Cypress Hill Bandit!"

Alex nodded. "OK." With that he turned the computer monitor to face the group standing in the middle of the room.

There, on the screen in vivid color, was the image of Alex standing beside a smiling man wearing a baseball cap. Around them lay piles of merchandise. The stranger was holding an almost-full mailbag bulging with various boxes and hardware supplies. At the bottom right-hand corner of the picture was imprinted the date and time, indicating that the image was recorded less than an hour before.

Sheriff Curtain's mouth dropped open as he edged toward the desk. "What . . . How . . ."

"Sir, this is the real Cypress Hill Bandit," the boy said pointing. "And that's me. I took this picture with a camera he'd stolen at the hardware store."

"He . . . he just let you take a photograph of him?"

"Well, he knew there was no film in the camera."

The sheriff looked over at Alex. "How did you take a picture without film?"

"Easy," the boy said, holding up the camera he'd been carrying in his pocket. A cord ran from the device to the back of the station computer. "It's a *digital* camera. Doesn't use film."

Rose walked over to her son and slipped her arm around his shoulders.

"One more thing, sir," Alex said as he pressed a key on the keyboard. "You really should see this too."

The image on the screen changed. As the group gathered around, a new picture scrolled across the monitor. It was a slightly blurry photograph of a man with a baseball cap holding a gun out in front of him. He had just pulled the trigger and a blossom of flame was glowing in front of the short barrel. Not more than five feet away, an old man with white hair was hurling himself through a doorway, arms outstretched, fists clenched, eyes focused on the gunman.

"He saved me," Alex whispered, studying the screen with the others. "He came back to save me."

Turning to face the sheriff, the boy added. "When they picked themselves up off the ground, the bandit heard you and your men coming so he jumped out through the window and ran away. If . . . if you'd like, I'll have my friend Kobe make some copies of this picture, and then you can show it to all the other police officers in the county so they'll know what he looks like and they can help you catch him."

Sheriff Curtain slumped down onto his chair. His shoulders sagged as he ran his fingers through his wet hair. "Alex . . . I'm sorry. I'm very sorry. I was accusing you . . ."

"That's OK," the boy interrupted. "You didn't know."

Deputy Frank strolled into the room and looked around. "What's going on?" he asked.

The officer at the desk looked up, his eyes tired, his face overcome with embarrassment. "Get the prisoner," he said. "He's not the Cypress Hill Bandit."

"OK," the deputy responded. "I'll bring him up just as soon as he's finished."

"Finished?"

"Yeah. He said he had to go to the bathroom. Should be done in a few minutes."

Sheriff Curtain closed his eyes and buried his face in his hands. "We can't even keep *innocent* people in our jail." He looked over at his deputies. "I'm going home to eat some very, very cold pizza. If anything else happens around here, don't call me. Just write up a report and put in on my desk. And Frank, go downstairs and fix the bathroom window."

"What's wrong with the bathroom window?"

"You'll see. Trust me, you'll see."

* * *

The summer sun glinted off the silver-and-brass surfaces of the trumpets, trombones, and saxophones as members of the Cypress Hill High School band swept down the street, filling the warm air with the thrilling sounds of a John Philip Sousa march. Behind them came a long, black Ford convertible with the mayor perched on the back seat, and beside him, waving to the smiling crowd, rode Miss West Virginia, the reigning state queen.

Men and women on horseback trotted along after the car, proudly showing off their handcrafted saddles and fancy riding clothes.

Members of the local fire station paraded by next, riding in their highly polished fire engine, blowing the horn and tapping the siren button in response to the excited shouts of the children fronting the gathering along each side of the street. It seemed as it everyone in town had turned out for the annual Summer Festival, glorying in the warm sunshine and waving small American flags.

The veterans of foreign wars marched by—old men in faded uniforms, honoring their branch of the armed forces with their grinning, patriotic presence.

Suddenly, the *rat-tat-tat* of a single drum could be heard. All eyes turned to see the Cypress Hill Pathfinder Club dressed in full regalia marching down the street, their feet stomping to the percussive rhythm of Shane's shiny drum. A cheer rose from the crowd when they recognized the boy on the front row, face beaming with pride, a brand-new badge bearing the image of a camera sewn on his sash. Alex waved shyly in response.

Alicia, marching beside him, and her drum-playing brother also sported the new badge on their sashes.

Alex felt as if his heart would burst. He'd done it. HE'D DONE IT! All his hard work had finally paid off. He and the other two members of the Honors Club had finished each and every requirement for their photography honor, and now they could show off the result of their efforts to the world.

The boy couldn't help but smile as he glanced over at Benson Park, its trees rising above the crowd. No, he hadn't been able to capture those silly squirrels with his camera. But Mr. Cho, along with everyone else in the Pathfinder club, had decided that taking a picture of the Cypress Hill Bandit in his natural surroundings—the warehouse—counted as a very valid wild animal shot.

Shane turned and glanced over at his sister and then Alex. The three nodded to one another, proud of their accomplishment, glad to be part of the parade, and happy that their goal had been reached.

As the Pathfinders marched by the entrance to the park, Mr. Cho gave the order, "Eyes right!" Every head in the group snapped in that direction. Then their leader ordered, "Sa . . . lute!"

Twenty-four hands rose to twenty-four foreheads just as the statue of Harry Benson came into view. The townspeople cheered, showing their appreciation as the club honored the great contribution their young war hero had provided so long ago.

As Alex marched to the drumbeat, hand held smartly above his right eye, he noticed a patch of white hair almost hidden in the crowd and a face that looked familiar. Lost in the assembled throng, one set of eyes held his in a gaze that revealed deep gratitude and the great sense of relief that comes from facing the truth and burying the ghosts of the past.

The boy remembered the words the old man had whispered to him as they rode to the police station that night. "Alex," he'd said, "a hero is simply a coward who has found something worth dying for. Don't ever forget that."

Alex smiled as he pressed his fingers into his forehead, holding his salute, staring into the eyes of someone who'd run away, and then returned to become the hero he'd always wanted to be.